Billionaire Cowboy's Conquest

by

Marie Tuhart

This is a work of fiction. Names, characters, places, and incidents are either the product of the author's imagination or are used fictitiously, and any resemblance to actual persons living or dead, business establishments, events, or locales, is entirely coincidental.

Billionaire Cowboy's Conquest

COPYRIGHT © Marie Tuhart

Contact Information: MarieTuhart@yahoo.com

Cover Art by *Diana Carlile*

ISBN: 978-0-9971800-2-2 (ebook)
ISBN: 978-0-9971800-3-9 (print)

Published in the United States of America

Dedication

As always, thank you to my critique partners for all their encouragement.

CHAPTER ONE

The purr of a low-pitched engine caused Hunter Knight to throw down the financial report he was reading. What idiot would be driving a sports car onto his ranch? He stood, and strode to the open door. A fire engine red vehicle with a fine sheen of dirt parked in front of the office.

Hunter lazed against the door jamb as the driver's door opened. A well-coiffed head of deep red hair appeared, then shoulders encased in a brilliant white shirt. He straightened, as the woman bent over and pulled something out of the vehicle.

His blood heated as it hadn't done in a long time at the sight of this gorgeous woman. He shook his head. He didn't even know who this person was. He waited while she slipped on a blue jacket on. The car door slammed and she marched around the car. Hunter stared at her.

The tailored business suit hugged her curves. His fingers itched to strip off her jacket and shirt at see what lay beneath as his gaze roamed her from head to toe.

His groin tightened as his gaze took in her mouth-watering curves, legs that went on forever, and delicate feet encased in high heels. His physical reaction to this woman startled him. He'd been celibate for far too long. That had to be it.

"Can I help you?" His voice sounded strangled to him.

She smiled and the impact went straight to his southern regions. "Hi. I'm looking for Susan."

"Susan isn't here right now." His sister had run into town to pick up a batch of new forms. Who was this woman? A memory of her tickled at the back of his brain.

"Oh." Her smile faltered a bit. "Well, I'm Jessica Sinclair, the new office manager."

"Hell no." What was his sister thinking? Yes, he agreed they needed help in the office. Yes, he told his sister to take care of it. But...this woman had city girl written all over her. She wouldn't last a day in the Texas summer heat. Jessica...wait a second. "Jessica Sinclair? As in my sister's college roommate and party girl?" He'd heard about Jessica's college exploits from his sister. Although he'd only met her briefly at graduation, he knew she was the last thing the Double K Ranch needed.

"I'm sorry?" A tiny frown appeared on her forehead, then her eyes widened with recognition.

"I can't believe Susan would hire you. I don't have time for amateurs."

Her lashes whisked down concealing her amber eyes, then lifted. Fire brewed in her gaze. Her shoulders stiffened. "I can assure you, Mr. Knight, I am a professional and I can run an office."

"Oh really." His gaze swept from those dainty feet, up her amazing body to her rosy face. "High heels have no place on my ranch."

Her lips pressed together. Damn if his groin

didn't tighten as he wondered how she would taste. *Cut it out, Knight. You don't need the complication a city woman would offer.* But play time might be worth the headache, if she wasn't off-limits.

"I talked to Susan last night. She assured me the office manager job was available and mine." She lifted her hand, shading her face from the hot Texas sun.

"It is." He wouldn't lie. He needed an office manager. "Come in out of the sun." The last thing he needed was her passing out from sun stroke. He turned and sauntered back to where he'd been sitting. A second later he heard the click, click, click of her heels on the floor. "Have a seat." He dropped down onto the leather chair.

Jessica glided over to the chair in front of the desk. The sunlight streaming through the window intertwined with her hair. Not red hair, but chestnut, almost a cinnamon color. Would it smell like his favorite scent?

Get a grip. City girls and country cowboys didn't mix. Hadn't his ex-wife proved that to him? His ex cared more about his money than him. He shook his head to clear away his morose thoughts and leaned back in the chair as she settled down onto hers.

"If the job is still available, then what is the problem?" Her tone was questioning, but firm.

"As I said, I need someone who can run this office." He ignored the way his blood heated as he stared at her.

"I assure you, I can handle the job." She sat with her back straight, shoulders tight, and fingers tangled in her lap.

"Which end of a horse do you keep clear of?" He tossed the question out.

"Both ends." Confidence oozed from her silky voice, and his annoyance level rose along with his awareness of her.

"What is an Angus?"

"Cattle."

"What do you do if a horse has colic?"

"Call a vet." She let out a sigh. "My understanding is I'm going to run the office, not be a ranch hand."

Hunter liked her spunk, but he didn't need a party girl distracting his workers. He leaned forward, forearms on the wooden desk. "Dallas is over a two-hour drive."

"And?" A note of impatience crept into her voice, and he bit back a grin.

"Longville doesn't have a mall, or a movie theater. Just a general store which is attached to the feed store. You'll be bored in a week."

Her head snapped up and fire flashed again in those amber eyes.

"Don't presume to tell me how I would feel." Her voice was tight, controlled as if she was holding onto her temper by a thread.

Let's see if he could break that thread and prove a city girl doesn't belong.

"You're a city girl. You don't belong on my ranch." His gazed raked over her body, lingering at her breasts straining against the fabric of her blouse.

"You know nothing about me, Mr. Knight."

"That's where you're wrong, Ms. Sinclair." He had her now. "Were you not the one who caused a riot at Alpha Delta House on the campus of Arizona University?"

She squirmed in her seat as a slight blush filled her cheeks.

"That wasn't my fault." Her voice was faint.

"And were you not the one who snuck into the boy's campus housing and stole the quarterback's jersey, which you then wore to the big game?"

Her chin dipped. "That was a long time ago. I'm a different person now."

He shook his head. "Tell me, what would you do if the barn was on fire?" He forced himself not to give into the haunted look on her face.

"Call the fire department."

"Wrong." He slapped his hand on the desk. Victory soared through is veins. "You'd get the horses out first, then call the fire department. You're unsuitable for this position."

Her shoulders slumped. Hunter sat waiting for her to either cry or storm out. The seconds ticked by, nothing happened. She took a deep breath. Her head rose, her spine stiffened, and she stared straight at him with fire blazing in her eyes.

"None of this has to do with an office job. I'm a darn good office manager. And from what Susan told me, you're desperate for help." She glanced around the room, noting the stacks of filing and overflowing paperwork on the desks, before her gaze settled back on him. "Frankly, Mr. Knight, I don't see applicants lined up for this job."

Hunter leaned back, rubbed his chin, and struggled not to smile. He liked how she fought back in spite of being a city girl. But she had a point. The ranch needed an office manager. Plus, if he was going to be able to ride in the National Finals Rodeo he needed to be out on the ranch keeping fit, not in the office doing paperwork he hated.

His hand slipped down and rubbed his right knee. Nothing like a few thousand pounds of bull to sideline his career for a few months. But how was he going to deal with Jessica? Technically, he needed her in the office in a professional capacity, but dang it, he wasn't ready to deal with another city girl. He also wasn't prepared for his attraction to her.

****

Jessica Sinclair sat on the hard chair, fighting her instincts to get up and run. She needed this job. The creditors were pounding at the door, thanks to her ex-fiancé Ned. Why had she ever trusted him? Somehow, Ned managed to max out every credit card she owned and got a personal line of credit in her name as well.

When she discovered Ned's deeds he was out of town on business, or so she thought. Until she called him and some woman answered with Ned yelling in the background for the woman to get her ass in bed.

Jess's fingers curled into her palms. The sharp sting of nails digging into her skin brought her back to the present. Yep, she needed this job. So she'd put up with Genghis Kahn if it got her the job.

But why was Hunter Knight so damn handsome? His wide shoulders begged a woman to lean against them. Jeans clung to his thighs and hips like a second skin. His raven hair reminded her of black satin sheets, and those, oh so, soulful brown eyes. They reminded her of fine chocolate, smooth and sinful.

This cowboy was too handsome, too cocky, and had no right to judge her based on her past. Yes, her impulsive nature had gotten her into trouble from time to time, but those days were over.

Okay, well, maybe not her impulsive nature. She struggled against slumping in the chair. Was it her fault she decked her boss when he goosed her at a work party? Was it her fault her boss's boss was there? Yep, that had gone over well. It wasn't like she would get a good reference from them.

Jess shifted her shoulders in small movements to ease the tension. She couldn't show Hunter any weakness. If she did, he'd exploit it like all men did. An oppressive silence filled the room. Jess fought not to rub her stomach to relieve her apprehension.

"I'll admit there's not a line of applicants." His whisky smooth voice slid over her skin in a subtle caress.

A long breath slipped from her lips. How could she overcome his objections? "How about a trial period?"

Where the hell had that come from? She ran the total in her meager checking account around in her brain. There was enough, if she was careful. She could pay the creditors pounding at her door their minimum until she got on her feet. Damn her ex-fiancé. She wouldn't be in this situation if it wasn't for him.

"A trial period?" His eyes narrowed as his gaze focused in on her.

A shiver swept up her spine. "Yes." She'd thrown down the gauntlet. "I'll work as the office manager for three months for room and board."

"And what happens at the end of that time?" His voice was calm.

"If I do a satisfactory job, you will pay me not only for the three months, but a nice bonus." Her stomach clenched. "If I fail, I leave without a word and you're out nothing."

Susan had told Jess the job came with a place to stay, plus Jess was welcome to eat in the main house. Jess held Hunter's gaze as the room went silent. He had nothing to lose, but she could lose everything. Not that she hadn't already.

"I accept your offer."

His tone was reluctant, but when the words penetrated her brain, she barely stopped herself from jumping up and dancing. Hunter rose to his feet and held out his hand. Her gaze shifted from his sensuous lips to his outstretched hand. She rose and put her hand in his. Rough skin caressed hers. Heat flowed from him, worming its way from her palm, up her arm, until it invaded her whole body. Alarm bells sounded in her head. This man was dangerous to her well-being.

"I'm glad we have that settled." Elephants took up residence in her stomach, but she ignored them. This would work out. She'd make sure of it.

A car door slammed. Jess jumped and Hunter released her hand.

"Susan, get in here," he yelled.

Susan. Oh thank goodness. Maybe she could get

away from this stubborn, handsome, sexy cowboy.

"You bellowed." Jess turned to see Susan breezed through the door.

Now that she'd seen them together, Jess noticed the family resemblance. Both had high cheek bones and firm chins. Susan's dark hair brushed her shoulders, but her eyes were a lighter shade of brown.

"Jess, you're here."

Susan pulled her in for a hug. It had been a while since Jess had seen her friend. They talked on the phone weekly, but it wasn't the same.

"Damn you look good, girl," Susan said.

"You don't look half bad either." Jess extracted herself from Susan's embrace.

"Clean living." Susan laughed. "Come on, I'll show you where you'll be staying." She grabbed Jess's arm and started to pull her out of the office.

Jess glanced back over her shoulder. Hunter stood there, arms crossed over his chest, a shit-eating grin on his face.

"I'll see you later," he said.

Why did his words send a shiver through her? She wasn't afraid of him, only how he made her feel.

"I'm so glad you're here." Susan said as they strode out into the bright sunshine.

"Me too." Jess pushed Hunter out of her mind as she paused beside her car. "I can't thank you enough for the job offer."

"No biggie." Susan waved her hand. "We really need the help."

"Yeah well, after Ned..."

"That piece of cow poop."

Jess burst out laughing at Susan's words.

"Come on, give me a ride in this baby." Susan opened the passenger door and slid in.

With a laugh, Jess climbed into the driver's seat and started her car. Chills crept over her skin as she looked around, even with the harsh sunlight coming through the windshield. How ironic. Her only hope for fixing her financial situation was working on a ranch that supplied stock to the rodeo where her father had been killed by a bull.

****

The next morning, Hunter paused beside the small cottage. His sister had volunteered him to oversee Jess moving in. He'd argued with Susan that he had plenty of things to do, but she pointed out the ranch hands were busy fixing fences and checking on the horses in the back pasture.

Since he couldn't ride a horse for long periods of time yet, he didn't have much choice other than to sit in the office and listen to his sister nag him. He rounded the corner of the cottage to see a local moving van pull up. Hunter frowned. It wasn't big van.

"Hi, Ty," John said as he climbed out of the cab.

"Hey." John ran a small moving company. Well, more than that, they moved furniture, but also livestock and anything else someone wanted transported.

The door of the cottage opened, Jessica walked out and down the two stairs. The white tank top molded to her breasts. A pair of purple short shorts showed off her long legs and tight ass. His groin tightened.

One of John's men let out a wolf whistle. Hunter frowned. Didn't she know better than to dress like that for a bunch of working men? This woman was going to attract trouble like honey drew bees.

"Miz Sinclair," John said.

"That's me." She held out her hand.

Did her tone have to be so sweet?

"Nice to meet you." John took the proffered hand. "It shouldn't take too long to unload."

"Thanks, I appreciate you storing everything."

She flashed a sexy smile as Hunter sauntered up to the pair. John was still holding her hand. "Miss Sinclair, a moment of your time, please," Hunter said.

John released her hand as Hunter took her by the elbow and led her inside the cottage.

"What do you think you're doing?" Annoyance tinged her voice at his manhandling.

"Do you have any clue what can happen to a woman who is dressed like you are?" He kept his voice low and tight.

"What are you talking about?"

"If you are going to work here, you can't be running around dressed like this." He fingered the strap on her tank top.

"Excuse me." Color rose to her cheeks, and she started to pull away.

Hunter grasped her shoulders. "There are very few women on the ranch."

"So?"

"This isn't a college dare, where you can sneak into the boys' dorm and steal the quarterback's team jersey. These are men. And while they've been warned you're off limits, you're still one hell of a temptation."

The color in her cheeks grew darker and her lips pressed together. She shifted her stance causing his hands to fall away from her shoulders. "I can handle myself."

"Want to bet?" Before the last word left his mouth, he caught her wrists and pinned them against the wall. He slid closer pressing his chest against her breasts. "So, what are you going to do now?"

She grinned. He barely sidestepped when she lifted her knee to his groin. But in doing that, he had to release one of her arms. Before he could recover, pain radiated from his gut and his breath whooshed out of him.

The little vixen drove her fist into his solar plexus in the move of a seasoned prize fighter.

"Satisfied?" A smug smile spread over her lips.

"I guess," he muttered. He'd concede it seemed she could take care of herself.

"Good. What are you doing here, anyway?" She stepped away from him and pushed a stray piece of hair behind her ear.

The pain diminished, and he could finally take a deep breath. "Susan sent me over." He leaned against the wall. "There are a few ground rules we need to get straight."

"What is it about men and rules?" She huffed out a breath.

"I am your boss."

"Fine." She wrinkled her nose at him. "I guess I

have no choice in the matter." Jess leaned against the wall and crossed her arms below her breasts.

Oh hell. The woman wasn't wearing a bra, he could see her nipples straining against the fabric. Hunter forced his gaze away from the tantalizing sight, but it didn't help.

"You need a different vehicle than that skateboard on wheels."

"I'm not getting rid of my car." She pushed away from the wall. "Isn't there a ranch vehicle I can use?"

He nodded. "For runs into town, yes."

"Okay, one rule settled. Next?"

Her saucy tone set his teeth on edge. "You will not run around the ranch dressed like this." His gaze raked over her bare skin. How would her skin feel beneath his palms? Silky smooth he imagined.

"I will dress professionally in the office, but what I wear on my own time is my business not yours."

She had a point, not that he liked it. "Agreed. No flirting or dating any of my ranch hands."

"As if." She threw her hands up in the air. "Dating a cowboy is the last thing I want to do."

"You don't like cowboys?" His eyebrows rose. Usually women were falling all over him and the other hands.

"Nothing against cowboys in general. It's the Y chromosome I have a problem with. I haven't found a man yet who is trustworthy or reliable."

His lips turned down. "That's not what I heard."

Jess froze. Her features went blank. "And what did year hear?" Her voice was strained.

"Susan mentioned you were a real party animal in

college and dated a lot of guys."

Her face flushed. "I did, but that was college."

"So, at the advanced age of twenty-six, or is it twenty-eight, you've outgrown your wild ways?"

"Experience is a wonderful cure." Anger filled her voice. "And for the record I'm twenty-eight."

"Don't use your experience on my men."

"Yes, sir." She snapped a saucy salute. "Anything else, sir?"

Her tone should have warned him off, but he enjoyed getting a rise out of her. She rose to the bait so easily. "How about a kiss?" Where the hell had that come from?

"Go kiss a cow." She turned and stomped away.

A smile crossed his lips. The material of her shorts clung to her rear and he had to shift his stance to ease the pressure in his groin. He wasn't going anywhere. He was going to make sure no man made a move on her unless it was him.

The thought sent a jolt through him. Had he changed his mind about this city girl? No. But flirting with her was fun. She was a pleasant distraction until he could ride again.

****

"Where the heck did I put those sheets?" Jess said out loud later that afternoon. The living room was a sea of cardboard boxes. She didn't remember having this much stuff. How would she fit it in this small quaint cottage.

"What are you searching for?"

Jess glanced up to see Hunter lounging against the door frame. Her tormentor was still here. No matter what she did, she couldn't get him to leave. He'd stayed and at times helped unload boxes into the cottage.

He pushed away from the wall and shuffled into the room. Jess had watched him more than she wanted to admit during the day. Now he was limping. How had he been hurt? She shook her head. It was none of her business. He was her boss, nothing more.

"I'm trying to find the box marked linens." She pushed another box marked miscellaneous out of her way. Hell, she should have gone though all these boxes before she left L.A.. She'd make a pile for donations and take them into Longville.

"Is this what you're looking for?" He held up a set of blue satin sheets.

"Yes." She let out a sigh. He would have to find those.

"Nice." His fingers caressed the silky material. A tremor started low in her belly.

"Thank you." She held her hand out for the sheets.

"Let me help you." He dropped them back into the box and picked it up. Before she could protest he was striding into her bedroom.

Drat the man. He couldn't leave her alone. The moving crew had left an hour ago, and yet he was still here. The last place she wanted him was in her bedroom. Thank goodness the bed was already put together.

"You've helped me enough for the day," she said following him into the room. "Why don't you go home?"

"I couldn't possibly leave until I've helped you make this lovely bed of yours." He stood next to the bed, with a sexy grin on his face, box in hand.

Jess groaned as the image of him in bed with her. She mentally slapped herself. Her one other luxury in life, a king sized bed. "I can make it myself."

"But you don't have to." He pulled the sheets out and set the box on the floor.

Jess let out a breath. Maybe, if the gods were smiling on her, he'd leave when they were finished.

They worked together silently. By the time they were done, sweat ran between her breasts. She brushed her hand over her forehead as her gaze met Hunter's. The heat increased. Oh lord, this was the last thing she needed, to be attracted to this cocky cowboy. Hadn't her mother's heartbreak over her cowboy husband shown Jess what a man like Hunter would do to her heart? Let alone her experience with Ned, her ex. Men were trouble.

"Could you please open the window?" she asked.

"Hot?" His muscles tightened and defined as he pushed the window up.

Her mouth dried out. "I'm a little warm." She fanned herself. The cool breeze soothed her flaming skin.

"Are you getting sick?" He crossed to stand in front of her. "It's not that hot today." He raised his hand to touch her forehead.

"Not sick, just warm." She shied away from his touch.

"Are you sure?" He advanced with a wanton gleam in his eyes.

"Yes," she whispered as she retreated until her back hit the wall. Oh crap, this wasn't good.

"What are you afraid of?" He moved with her.

"No...nothing." She silently cursed the stutter.

"Liar." He placed his palms against the wall, trapping her.

Her spine molded to the wall behind her as his breath caressed her cheeks. A pulse began deep within her core, and traveled through her veins.

No, she couldn't afford to let him affect her like this. "I am not a liar." She tilted her head back to stare him in the eye. She wouldn't show this man weakness. Men like him took joy in exploiting weakness in a woman.

He leaned closer, his lips scant inches from hers. The warmth of his skin seeped through her shirt to her breasts. It wasn't fair. She couldn't be attracted to him. She arched her neck.

"Hunter."

Her body jolted at an unknown man's voice. "Oh God," Jess whispered. She held her breath as Hunter's mouth hovered above hers, then he dropped a kiss on the end of her nose before stepping away.

"Be right out, Chris," he yelled.

Jess took a deep breath trying to calm her racing heart.

"Ranch hand. Since we're through for the moment, I'll see what Chris wants then head for a shower," Hunter said.

"Good idea." Yeah, she needed a cold shower to clear her muddled brain.

"Want to share that shower?"

Her head jerked up to see him with a sexy grin on his face. "Not today, cowboy."

"I'll take a rain check then." He paused next to her. "And I plan to collect."

Jess watched him saunter out of the room, then she fell onto the newly made bed as her knees gave out. Oh dear Lord, what was she going to do? She'd best remember he was toying with her to scare her off the ranch. That's all it was. Because no way in hell would she succumb to her attraction to Hunter Knight.

****

Hunter wiped the sweat off his brow. He'd fought to control his reaction to Jess while they made the bed. When she bent over to tuck in the cover, her round derriere begged for his caress.

He needed a shower all right. A cold one. He enjoyed pushing Jessica's buttons, but he hadn't expected his own reaction to be so intense. When was the last time he'd been with a woman? A while, well over a year. Between being on the rodeo circuit and the ranch he hadn't had time for a quality relationship.

Jessica was all woman. A little aggressive flirting wasn't going to scare her away. Nope. She'd fight him the entire way, making him work for success. A grin spread across his lips. Getting her off his ranch was going to be fun.

She'd even admitted she'd liked to party and play. He remembered all the stories Susan told him about Jess and her wild ways. She might not want to get involved with him, but she didn't tell him to take a hike either.

Her amber eyes had filled with desire when he

was close to her. She was as affected as he was by the intimacy of her bedroom. And as for driving her from the ranch? He was toeing a fine line here. Susan was technically Jessica's boss. He also owned the ranch though, and he'd get rid of a city girl as a matter of survival.

"Hey, Hunter," yelled Chris.

"What's up, Chris?"

"Wild Thing is acting up again."

Well, so much for a shower. He followed Chris out to the pasture where Wild Thing stomped around, head held high, nostrils flaring and his eyes wild. Damn, his rankest bull was not having a good day.

He motioned Chris to head further down the fence line as he strode to the gate where two other hands waited with a horse. Even with his bum knee, he could ride for short periods of time. Swinging himself into the saddle, he took the reins and nodded.

The ranch hands opened the gate, and the horse trotted in. Hunter took the rope one of the cowboys held out to him. Wild Thing was going to breed if it was the last thing that damn bull ever did. Hunter held up his hand, and two other cowboys on horseback entered the area. Time to wrangle up this bull. He adjusted the rope and guided the horse with his knees. The horse hadn't taken three steps when Wild Things gaze zeroed in on him and the bull charged.

CHAPTER TWO

Jess wiped her hand down her jeans before she entered the office the next morning. She could do this. After catching up with Susan over dinner last night, she'd relaxed more. But this morning, Jess was again unsettled by Hunter.

"He's just a man," she whispered to herself. Yes, but what a man he was. Up close, she'd seen his well-defined muscles from working the ranch. Her fingers itched to traces those muscles, to feel their strength.

She shook her head. Thoughts like that would get her into trouble. She didn't need Hunter or any man in her life. This was about starting over, not making the same mistakes.

"Good morning, Jess," said Susan as she strode into the office. "You're early."

"Not for me." It was just a little after seven. Jess did her best work in the mornings before anyone else could disturb her. "I don't sleep much past six anymore."

"You were always an early bird, even when you partied late at night." Susan tilted her brunette head.

"And you loved to sleep in until noon."

Susan laughed. "I miss those days. There's coffee, bagels, and cream cheese in the break room. If you want something more, I can run down to the bunkhouse, and ask Paddy to fix you up a plate."

"Paddy?" Jess pictured a big Irish man with a white beard.

"He's the bunkhouse cook."

"Bagels are fine." She usually didn't eat much for breakfast.

"Great. I'll give you the nickel tour." Susan smiled. "Let's start with the break room."

Jess's nerves settled down as Susan showed her around. The office building was larger than she realized. Three offices, the reception area, supply room, and break room. There was also a large room which held a mahogany table with big comfortable chairs. Connected to the conference room, as Jess had dubbed it, was what she could only call a display room.

Pictures of horses and bulls graced the walls, along with awards. Best of show. Best of breed. Best bloodline. Horse trainer of the year. Stock contractor of the year. NFR champion bull rider...Jess's breath caught in her throat. Hunter's name was on the plaque.

"Hunter used to ride bulls?" Her stomach clenched.

"He still does." Susan reached up and ran her fingers over the frame.

"You mean he doesn't just train the horses?" Jess fought the churning in her tummy.

"No," Susan laughed. "Hunter does train the horses and the bulls, but he's also a bull rider. He'd be out on the circuit right now, but isn't because he hurt his leg."

"Hurt?" Ice filled her veins. It was bad enough

her dreams from last night were filled with him, but to find out he risked his life riding bulls, that alone put the kibosh on any relationship they might have.

Relationship? What was she thinking? She couldn't...wouldn't have a relationship with Hunter. Not a bull rider.

"You okay?"

Jess pulled herself together. "Yeah, just hungry."

"Come on, let's get a bagel and coffee, then I'll show you your office."

Jess followed Susan to the break room where she poured herself a cup of coffee, and nibbled on a bagel.

"The fridge is fully stocked, so you can get lunch out of it, or again go see Paddy." Susan said, leading Jess down a hallway. "Your office is next to Hunter's. Chris, the ranch manager is across from both of you. I'm out front."

"I have my own office?" This she didn't expect.

"Of course." Susan pushed open the oak door. "I usually answer the phones in the morning, greet clients and get them settled. In the afternoon, if I'm needed, like right now with us being short-handed, I'll go help with the horses."

"So you want me to get the phones in the afternoon?" Jess stepped into the room. Her world stopped spinning and locked into a stationary orbit. Office work settled her like nothing else.

Across the room from the door, an executive cherry wood desk occupied the large space. A state of the art computer sat on the desk along with several stacks of files. One wall held file cabinets, and the other wall had an empty bookcase.

"Like it?" Susan asked.

"Love it." The walls were bare. Jess ran through her head the pictures she'd brought with her. So much had been in storage when she lived with Ned because it didn't fit in with his so-called lifestyle.

"Good. Computer is hooked up to our network, the printer is in the supply room. I set your profile up already with a temporary password of your name."

"I can see that IT degree of yours came in handy." Jess's lips turned up at Susan's enthusiasm.

"Yeah." Susan grinned. "Hey how is baby brother Ben doing?"

Pride swelled in Jess at the mention of her brother. "He's doing great. I called him last night to let him know where to find me. He's enjoying medical school and he told me he picked up a part-time job on weekends."

"Wow, that must be hard."

"I know, I told him not to, but he says it gives him good experience." She didn't want him working, but she couldn't stop him. Thank goodness this year's payment for his classes was already done or she'd be in real trouble. Another reason why she had to make things work out at the ranch.

"I'll let you get settled. The first set of files are informational for you. If you need anything just holler." Susan strolled out.

Jess made her way over to the desk. Using a napkin, she placed her coffee cup on it and then sat down in the executive leather chair. She let out a sigh. She could get used to this kind of luxury. In her old office she just had a plain old secretary's chair.

She reached over and turned on the computer. The log-in screen came up, she typed in her name, then her name for her password. The desktop icons appeared and Jess went to work.

Three hours later, she had a better idea of what it took to run a ranch of this size. The Double K was over eight hundred acres. She could never have imagined it was so big.

She'd read files about the ranch. They trained horses for both saddle bronc and bareback riding. They also had an area for team ropers to train. They raised calves for calf roping, and of course the bulls.

Jess found this wasn't a typical office job. Yes, while she'd manage the office, there was a lot of recordkeeping. Vaccinations for all the animals, stud records, breeding records, injuries, plus a list of the all rodeos where they were stock contractors. Her job wouldn't be dull. Perfect, because she could use all her concentration to shove Hunter out of her mind.

She pushed her chair back and stood. Arms over her head, Jess stretched. A cup of coffee and a snack and then she'd be ready to tackle the financials of the ranch. Jess made her way to the small break room and poured herself a cup of coffee. She sipped it before a smile crept over her lips at the sight of a fruit bowl on the counter.

Susan remembered she loved having fruit as a snack. Snatching up an apple and a banana, Jess headed back to her office only to stop dead in the doorway.

Hunter was lounging against her desk. Well, so much for having a peaceful afternoon.

"What can I do for you?" she asked skirting around the opposite side of the desk. A grin played around his lips and an icy edge of awareness slid up her spine.

"I'm here to take you on a tour of the ranch."

"Whatever for?" The words slipped out of her before she could stop them.

The grin turned into a slight frown. "You need to know the layout in order to show clients around when necessary."

"Show clients?" She wrinkled her nose. "When did that become part of my job description?"

"If you're not willing to do the job you've been hired for, then tell me now so we can find someone else."

"That's not what I'm saying." Drat the man.

"Hey, what are you two arguing about?" Susan stuck her head into Jess's office.

"I was telling Jess I was here to take her on a tour of the ranch."

"Great idea." Susan's smile faded when she looked at Jess. "Did I forget to mention that when I told you about the job?"

"Yes." Jess fought against a sigh. She'd just have to buck it up and go on the tour. She could handle his presence. "I guess there's no time like the present." Finishing off her coffee, she set the mug on her desk.

"Do you have a hat?" he asked as he straightened from where he was lounging. "Your complexion is very fair and our sun is hot."

"I have an extra one." Susan disappeared only to return in a minute with a cowboy hat in her hand.

"Here this should work."

Jess took the hat from Susan's hand and plopped it down on her head.

Hunter shook his head. "Shall we get started?" He gestured for Jess to precede him out of the office.

"Have fun," Susan said as they walked out of the office.

****

Hunter allowed his gaze to skim over Jess's body. Her blouse was light but enough to protect her from the sun. At least she was wearing jeans today. He stared at her shoes. Sneakers. Those wouldn't do.

"You need a pair of boots." He cupped her elbow in his hand and began guiding her to the small shed next to the office.

"What?" Her head snapped up to stare at him.

"Boots. Cowboy boots to be exact." He punched in the code to the lock and opened the door on the shed, and tugged her inside. "What size?"

"This isn't necessary." She crossed her arms over her breasts.

"I'm asking for your shoe size, not your bra size. Not that I wouldn't mind finding it out in a more intimate setting."

Her mouth dropped open. "In your dreams, cowboy."

Hunter stood there staring at her until she let out a sigh.

"Fine. Size eight, wide, please." She scuffed the toe of her sneaker against the floor.

He hid a grin. She apparently didn't like her shoe size, but he sure did. He'd caught a glimpse of those slim ankles and silky skin. He went over to the rack of boots they kept for clients and selected a pair.

"The boots here are for clients to use. There are hazards on the ranch and we don't want anyone getting hurt." He gestured at the bench and Jess sat. Hunter snagged the small stool, put it in front of her, and sank onto it. He reached for her leg.

"There's no need, I can put them on." She turned away from him.

"I'm sure you can, but I want to make sure they fit." He cupped her heel in his palm, then lifted her leg until her calf rested on his thigh. He unlaced her sneaker, slipped it off and set it on the bench next to her.

Hunter slid her jeans up to her calf. Her shiver almost had him smiling. Picking up the boot, he worked it over her toes and ankle until it was seated before he smoothed the denim back into place.

His fingers lingered on her calf, massaging the tense muscles there. Jess shifted and their gazes collided. Amber eyes blazed as his fingers caressed her through the fabric of her pants. He was playing with fire and didn't mind getting burned.

The flame in her eyes grew brighter, hotter as he moved his hand from her calf to her knee, then continuing until he reached her thigh. The pads of his fingers gently caressed her. He itched to remove her clothing and feel her soft silky skin.

When Jess shifted in her seat, Hunter slipped her foot to the floor and walked his fingers over her hips, to her waist, to rest beneath her breasts. Unable to help himself, his palm cupped her breast. She inhaled.

But she didn't stop him. Her nipple pebbled at his touch. Anticipation shimmered between them.

"Got a minute, Hunter."

The male voice shattered the mood. Jess drew in a sharp breath. Her hands on his shoulders pushed him away.

"In here." Hunter rose, praying no one would notice how stiffly he was moving. Wild Thing's tantrum yesterday. He'd had a narrow miss of being gored and his being on a horse strained his knee muscles.

"Sorry," Chris said, glancing at Jess sitting on the bench putting on the second boot.

"No problem, just outfitting our new office manager." Hunter glanced at her. "Jess, meet Chris, my right hand man. Chris, Jess."

"Hi, Chris." Jess stood up and held out her hand.

They shook hands, but Hunter didn't miss the way Chris's gaze appraised Jess.

"What's up?" Hunter asked, moving to Jess's side, a possessive streak curled in his gut.

"Rainey's acting skittish. We need your help."

"Okay, I'll be right down."

"Great. Miss Jess." Chris touched his hat before sauntering out the door.

"Don't flirt with my men."

"What? I only shook his hand." Jess glared at him, but the heat in her gaze was more anger not passion. "Get an eye exam, you're seeing things."

"You're off limits to my men. Remember?" He grasped her hand. "Now let's go see what the problem with Rainey is."

What had happened to her? Jess was angry with Hunter's possessiveness but here she was letting him lead her across the grounds. Had Hunter woven some sort of spell over her?

It had started out as him helping her with the boots, but the second he touched her, an explosion went off within her body. She expected him to be rough, but instead his touch was gentle, almost loving. Those calloused hands made her skin tingle.

And it shook her to the core. Her reaction wasn't one she wanted to have. While Hunter wasn't technically her boss, as she reported to Susan, he did own the ranch so that made him her boss. But even now, as she fell a step behind him, her gaze took in the way his jeans stretched over his butt, and his shirt taunt across his wide shoulders.

She trembled as she remembered the heat from his skin invading her skin when his hand cupped her breast. The anticipation flowing through her veins when the tips of his fingers moved to cover her nipple. Heat pooled low in her belly despite her declaration of not wanting him. She wasn't as immune as she needed to be.

Jess tripped over her own feet. Stop it. This line of thought wasn't productive. Besides, she didn't want a man in her life, let alone a rodeo cowboy.

"Wait here," Hunter said, dropping her hand at the entrance to the barn.

Jess watched him stride away, with a slight limp, through the big open double doors of the barn. The familiar smell of hay and horse flesh engulfed her. Her heart pounded. Her clammy fingers curled into her palms.

The memory of her father on his favorite horse cut through her mind. How could she have forgotten those smells? When she was a little girl, she'd loved them. It meant she was able to spend time with her dad. She'd loved being with him, watching him ride a horse. That wasn't dangerous. Life had been simpler then. Idyllic.

"Come in, Jess."

Hunter's voice brought her out of her memories. She stepped into the coolness of the barn. Her eyes adjusted to the muted light. There were stalls on both sides of the barn. One side of the barn held horses, some with their heads hanging out over the stall doors. On the other side, the barn wall was open to a large pasture and there was a big snort made Jess jump.

"It's okay." Hunter touched her shoulder. "It's just Outrageous making a fuss."

She couldn't help smiling. "Outrageous. Funny name for a horse."

"He's not a horse." Hunter pointed and she gazed through the stall door. There on the other side, just outside the wall, was a bull. A massive bull. The creature snorted again, sending her heart into a frantic gallop. "He's one of the bulls," Hunter continued speaking like a proud owner, unaware of the quake crumbling her courage to pieces. "He got a little too rambunctious a couple of days ago, so we've had to put him here in the pasture connected to the barn."

Jess wrapped her arms around her waist as her stomach churned. The bull turned his unfathomable eyes in her direction. Memories bombarded her, the roar of the crowd, the snorting of the bull, then the utter silence.

She couldn't tear her gaze away from this murderous beast. Her vision centered on this...killer. She couldn't do this. She couldn't be this close to the kind of animal that killed her dad. The experience was too much. She wrenched away from Hunter and ran from the barn.

CHAPTER THREE

Jess leaned her butt against the barn wall, hands on thighs gulping in air. *It's okay.* She tried to convince herself, but failed.

"Head between your knees." Hunter placed a hand against the back of her neck, urging her head down.

She bent further down because anything was better than meeting his gaze. Damn, she'd probably blown this job. Forcing the thought away, she concentrated on getting her breathing under control. She fought to push the memories of her father's death back into the box in the back of her mind where they belonged.

Jess closed her eyes and concentrated on breathing in and out. She imagined a cool calm ocean, its waves gently washing over her skin, caressing her body, and when the waves receded all her troubles went with the tide.

"Better?" Hunter asked, concern in his voice.

"Yes." She rose, thanking her lucky stars she hadn't tossed her cookies.

"What happened?"

"I'm not sure." She wasn't about to tell him the truth. If she did, he'd have her bundled up and thrown off his ranch in record time. She needed this job to pay off her debts, to start a new life.

"Let's get you inside." He leaned down and scooped her into his arms.

"I can walk," she protested, but her arms looped around his neck for balance all while trying to ignore his solid muscles.

"Susan would have my head if something happened to you on your first day." His long strides ate up the distance from the stable, until they arrived at what looked like a small cabin. And it wasn't her cabin.

"That isn't my place."

"No, it's mine. I let Susan have the main house and I took the cabin." He shouldered open the door. The fear of the bull melted away in his arms and she couldn't muster the will to insist he continue to her own cabin. "You need to lie down."

Before she could object, he was striding down the brightly decorated hall into a very masculine bedroom, where he placed her on the dark green bedspread.

"Don't move," he ordered before moving away.

Disregarding his command she threw her legs over the side of the bed the second he was out of sight. She couldn't stay here. She tried to stand up.

He reappeared, dropped a washcloth onto the dark wood nightstand, and put his hands on her shoulders. "I said don't move."

"I'm all right." She tried to ignore the warmth of his skin seeping into her bones.

"Lie down." The pressure of his hands on her shoulders, forced her to sit and then lie back on the mattress. He picked up the washcloth and placed it on her forehead.

"Quit fussing." She hated being fussed over. She was stronger than this.

"Is that what you think I'm doing?" His hip brushed hers as he sat on the mattress. Heat flared deep within in her. His watchful gaze warmed her heart. He was worried about her.

"I already feel better."

"Good. Want to tell me what happened?"

She lowered her gaze. She hated lying, but she couldn't afford to tell him the truth. Doing that was a one-way ticket to the unemployment line. She could deal with it, but the sight of the bull and the rush of painful memories had caught her by surprise. She was prepared for the next time. "I don't know."

"Did you eat this morning?"

His demand was a relief. "A bagel." She wasn't much of breakfast eater, but food wasn't the issue.

"Damn it, Jess." He sprung off the bed and started pacing. "Of all the stupid things to do."

"You don't have to yell." Let him think the lack of food was the reason for her reaction. It was better than the alternative.

"Yelling seems the only way to get through to you. From now on, you will join me for breakfast."

"I will not." Oh, no. He wasn't going to order her around. No way.

"Don't argue with me." He stopped his pacing and stared down at her. His commanding presence ate up all the space around them. "I'm going to fix you something to eat, and if you so much as set one toe out of that bed without my permission, I promise you'll regret it."

"Hunter," she started, but he'd already stomped out of the room. The man was impossible. She fought equal amounts of amusement, frustration and pleasure.

****

Hunter slammed the frying pan on the stove before storming over to the refrigerator. What was wrong with her, skipping breakfast? Breakfast was the most important meal especially on a ranch. Only a city girl would make the mistake of skipping a meal.

He quickly fixed a ham and cheese omelet, plus some toast. His kitchen was custom-built for maximum efficiency. The wide stainless steel fridge and cherry cabinets were always stocked with the essentials. Once the food was cooked, he put it on a plate, poured a glass of milk and arranged everything on a tray then carried it back to the bedroom.

He was pleased to find Jess was still in bed as he left her. By the mutinous expression on her face she wasn't happy about his orders, but at least she listened. She sat up when he approached the bed.

"I want you to eat every bite," he said, setting the tray over her lap.

"But—"

"Not negotiable. You are not leaving this bed until you eat everything on that tray."

She looked at the plate in front of her. "I'm a vegetarian."

Surprised flashed through his body. "Figures." He let out a frustrated sigh.

"I'm kidding." Picking up the fork and taking a big bite of the omelet. Within five minutes she'd finished everything he'd brought.

"Thank you," she said. "I was hungry after all."

"You're welcome." He lifted the tray and set it on the floor out of the way. "I have breakfast at six-thirty every morning. Starting tomorrow, I expect you here to eat."

Her eyes widened. "That's not necessary. I'll eat."

"If I remember, meals were included in our deal" His voice was soft as he reached over and tucked a strand of hair behind her ear.

She angled her head away from his touch. "I'm feeling better. I know you have work to do and I should get back to the office."

"In a minute."

Her gaze darted away from his. What was she hiding? Was she affected by his touch? He lifted her hand from where it rested on the bedspread, and resumed his seat on the mattress. When she tried to tug her hand away, he bit back a grin. He grasped her wrist and cradled her hand in his lap, drawing circles on her forearm with his nail. She shivered.

"Work..." Her word trailed off as he slid his fingers up her arm to her shoulder, lightly caressing her skin.

"Work can wait," he said, his face inches from her. His brain warned him this wasn't a good idea, but he ignored it.

His index finger traced her lips and she started breathing in rapid pulses. His own heart rate sped up. Her soft mouth against the skin of his fingers shot arrows of arousal through him.

"Hunter." Her voice was subdued. She placed a hand on his chest. It took him a second to realize she was trying to push him away.

"Easy, girl," he said, his tone deep and calming. It was a tone he used when he was trying to calm a nervous filly. In a way he was. He allowed her to push him back, moving the hand in his lap until it rested against his pounding heart.

"This is what you do to me."

She snatched her hand back as if she'd been burned. "This is inappropriate, Mr. Knight."

He'd smile, but she did have a point. Damn, what was wrong with him that he couldn't stay away from some wisp of a city girl? Hunter pushed to his feet and stared down at her. "Meet me at the front door in five minutes and we'll continue our tour." He picked up the tray and marched from the room. Five minutes to calm his wild thoughts.

Jess couldn't move if she wanted to. It was as if all her bones had melted the second Hunter touched her. My God, his lingering masculine scent filled the air. How did he manage to get her so off guard? Was it something he was born with? Or did he cultivate it? And how fair was it? She unraveled so easily around him.

She didn't want to like Hunter. He was a hard-ass cowboy, but damn he could be nice too. And his overbearing behavior didn't turn her off like it should. Someone in heaven had a sick sense of humor to throw the temptation of Hunter Knight in her lap so soon after the disaster with Ned. There was a sobering thought. She shook her head to clear the last of the sensual cobwebs. She hadn't survived tropical storm Ned to be done in by hurricane Hunter.

And being in Hunter's bed wasn't helping the issue. She rose and marched into the bathroom. She turned on the cold water and splashed some on her face before staring at her reflection.

He's your boss. The last thing she needed was to get involved with him. One false step and Hunter would fire her. No second chances, no hope to cash in on the bonus at the end of her trial period. She needed to remember that. She needed this job. Priorities. Goals. Reality. Time to focus on her job and not her wild attraction for the boss.

Drying her face, she finger-combed her hair, straightened her blouse and lifted her chin. No more. She would remain professional through the rest of the tour. With that in mind she strode to the front door where Hunter was waiting for her.

****

"The bulls in this paddock are part of the rodeo stock."

Jess nodded, fighting with all her mental strength to focus on Hunter's words and not the big hulking bulls milling around behind a fence she worried wouldn't hold them back if they charged. Her gaze kept straying to Hunter's tight butt in those sexy, faded jeans. Why endanger his life on these beasts, when he could make millions as a model?

Hunter stopped next to the fence and Jess followed suit, her gaze glued to the bulls as Hunter continued to tell her how beautiful they were. The old cliché "beauty is in the eye of the beholder" went through her mind. To her, these creatures were anything but beautiful. They were killers.

She cringed as one of the bulls ambled closer. Hunter took her hand in his. "It's okay." He cupped her elbow and turned her away. "Bulls can be intimidating. Let me show you some better looking stock."

Heat seared her skin, and wormed its way through her body at his touch. Why couldn't she control her body's reaction to this man? She sighed as they stopped at another fence line. He was so sweet, thinking she needed to see better looking stock. He had no idea. Let's see if she could keep it that way.

"Now these ladies are real beauties." He gestured with his hand, his chest thrust out, and his voice laced with pride.

Jess glanced up at the horses. She blew out a breath. Okay, horses she could handle. "Yes, they are," she murmured as a brown horse whinnied, broke away from the group, and trotted up to them.

A large head with a white diamond under the forelock was thrust over the fence and Hunter laughed. "This is Willa." He reached out and patted the horse's neck. "She's a four-year-old quarter horse."

The horse bared its teeth and nipped at Hunter's hand and Jess's heart leapt into her throat.

"Sorry girl." Hunter rubbed the horse's nose. "I don't have any treats right now. These quarter horses are great around children. They're gentle and calm."

"You're the expert." She rolled her head trying to loosen her neck muscles. *These are horses, they're not as dangerous as bulls.*

"And soon you'll be an expert too."

"I don't know about that. Unless you plan to assign one of them as my assistant in the office." She grinned at him to let him know she was joking. "But I'm sure I'll learn a lot." In the office, not on the ranch itself. She sneezed.

"Bless you."

"Thanks." Jess sniffled and wiggled her nose.

"Come pet Willa."

"No thanks." Jess stepped back. "I think I'm allergic." She rubbed her nose. Part of her was aware she was being unreasonable. She'd dealt with horses before her father died. Apprehension seized her, leaving her stomach in knots.

Usually horses didn't bother her. So why was she so fearful of them now? Had she made a mistake insisting she was cut out for this job? No, she couldn't think like that. Without references, what choice did she have? Damn her ex-boss, and damn Ned, too. If she didn't know better, she'd swear both men conspired to ruin her life.

Hunter shrugged and gave Willa one last pat on the nose before turning to Jess. "Why don't we head back to the office and I'll give you a short lesson on how to read the vet records."

"Sounds good." Thank goodness they getting away from the stock. Her muscles ached from tension and keeping her fear from overtaking was harder than she'd expected.

****

"Were you able to understand our system this

morning?" Hunter pulled up a chair next to hers once they were in her office.

"Yes. You've got a pretty standard database system." She logged in and brought up the vet records. "You have them categorized by breed and name. It's easy enough to bring up the vaccinations, illnesses, breeding and births." Her fingers danced along the keys bringing up the records on Willa.

"Great. We'll also need you to create a new database for when buyers are coming out to look at the stock, who they looked at, and if they bought. Also, one to update which stock we're using at which rodeo."

"I think I can handle it as long as I get the information from you or the ranch hands." Her confidence returned to her in waves. She was in her element now.

"We'll see." He pushed back his chair. "Be right back."

Jess frowned. What was going on? There was something in his voice that put her on alert. Hunter walked back into the room with a five-inch stack of paper. He dropped it onto her desk.

"What's that?" Her stomach sank.

"Our client database. None of us have had time to change it from paper to computer. One of the reasons we needed an office manager."

"More like a data entry person," Jess muttered, grabbing the first sheet of paper. She read it over quickly. Pretty standard stuff. It would just take her a while to build a searchable database. "You're going to make me work hard for the bonus money, aren't you?" She gave the pile a wary glance.

"Yep. You negotiated your salary and bonus. You're going to earn every penny."

She rubbed her forehead. "I can handle it."

"I'll be down at stable three if you need anything." With that he sauntered from the room.

Jess breathed a sigh of relief. She refused to accept she was over her head. All she had to do was concentrate on work without his presence titillating her senses. Maybe she had a chance of this thing working out. The job, not Hunter.

****

Sun filtered in from the windows set high to allow in light but keep the stable cool. Fans kept the air circulating, their motors mixing with the pleasant shuffling, stamping and snorting sounds of a dozen horses. The smell of horse sweat and straw was the best perfume known to man.

"Tour go okay?" Chris asked, leaning against the stall wall.

"Fine." Hunter ran his hands over Rainey's stomach, feeling the slight bulge beneath the smooth warm coat. "Looks like the breeding took hold."

"Yeah, that's why I wanted you to come and check on her. I think we should call the vet."

"Not a bad idea." He wanted to confirm their suspicions. The horse belonged to a fellow rodeo buddy and the foal was a present for his daughter.

"I'll get on it." Chris paused and stared at Hunter. "Deke said Jess almost passed out earlier. Is she okay?"

"Yeah." Hunter shut and locked the stall door.

"The woman didn't eat breakfast. I don't know why city women feel they have to be skinnier than a pencil." Hunter watched Chris for a reaction. He knew the foreman was in love with his sister, but he wouldn't tolerate any inkling toward Jess. At all. He scrubbed his neck. It wasn't good for the ranch.

"Maybe because some men want their women like that."

"Give me a break, Chris. When I go to bed with a woman, I want more than a stick sleeping next to me."

"Thinking about bedding the new office manager already?"

Hell, yes, he wanted to bed Jess. She filled his mind like no other woman. Not even his ex-wife Shana had done that. Jess gave as good as she got. She was a sensual challenge, one he was going to conquer.

"Your silence doesn't fool me. I've seen the way you watch her every move."

"She's an outsider. I won't get involved with another city woman." At least not seriously. A tumble in bed maybe.

Chris grinned at him. "Yeah. We'll see about that."

****

Later that night, Hunter stared up at the star-filled sky. He couldn't sleep and loved this time of night, not too cold, but not too warm. He sat out by the pool, letting the peace of the night soothe his tired mind and body.

His leg ached and a few laps in the pool would help. He slipped the towel from around his waist and dove into the water. The water was cool and soothing against his naked body.

The first few strokes, his leg protested, then the muscles began to stretch and warm up. Three more months. That's how long Doc said he had to stay off the rodeo circuit. As he did laps, Hunter calculated his points and where he would be at that time.

Thankfully, he'd had a great season up until that bull bucked just right. Even with the forced time off, he was still in the top ten and would stay there. His goal now was to finish healing and win the National Finals Rodeo.

Bull riding was a young man's game. Not that he was old by any means, but at thirty the hard life was catching up with him. Doc had already reminded him. One more concussion and he was out of the game forever. He'd been careful this year. No one could have predicted that bull would do a roundabout and Hunter would lose his balance and go flying.

It hadn't been a graceful exit. He'd landed hard on his right leg. Luckily he didn't break it, but he'd crumpled to the ground under the pain. He'd all but torn the ligaments in his knee. Rest was the only cure.

He'd rested for the first two months, but now he was itching to ride again. But he had responsibilities on the ranch. They were short-handed and Hunter filled in as much as possible. After twenty laps, he turned onto his back and floated.

His sister did as much as she could, but still, he felt the burden on his shoulders alone. He wished he had someone to share these midnight swims with. Someone to talk about the triumphs and frustrations of the day. Someone who he could snuggled up to in the middle of the night.

Whoa, where were these thoughts coming from? After his horrible divorce from Shana, he wasn't sure he ever wanted another woman in his life, but the image of Jess rose in his mind. There was something about her. She pushed into his life, first by convincing him to hire her and now by the pull of attraction he couldn't deny.

He climbed out of the pool and grabbed the towel. There was no room for a woman in his life. A casual fling, yes. Hot sex to ease the pressure building inside him, yes. But a committed relationship? No way. He'd had enough. Thank goodness he'd had a pre-nup with Shana. She'd wanted nothing more than his money.

Hunter shook his head. The problem was, he had too much time on his hands. Normally he was so tired at the end of the day that he ate dinner, read a bit, then fell fast asleep. Well, that would change. With Jess running the office, he could get back out on the ranch with his men and do his share of the workload, if his knee cooperated.

And Jess was already doing a fine job at running the office despite him being so hard on her and trying to trip her up. A twinge of remorse stuck him in the gut. Maybe he shouldn't be so hard on her.

A flash of light caught his eye. He turned. From here by the pool, he had a perfect view of Jess's cottage. It was late. Was she having trouble sleeping, too? The temptation to walk over and see if she was okay overwhelmed him, but he shoved it away.

Nothing could come of him going to see her

tonight. He sat down on the lounger, but kept his eyes on her place. A few minutes later, Jess emerged. His gut tightened. Did she have anything on? He sat up. Fabric lifted in the light breeze. Oh thank God she had something on.

He ran a hand through his wet hair as temptation gnawed at him. Jess had no idea he could see her from his pool, and he'd left his lights off so there was no reason for her not to believe she wasn't alone.

Her creamy skin was a beacon in the moon light. His fingers itched to touch her soft skin. Need curled in his belly, unfettered and primal. How would she feel underneath his body? Was she a quiet lover? Or a screamer? Lust washed over him leaving him hot and erect.

He rose from the lounger and took two steps before coming to a dead stop. What the hell? No. He would not go to her. Nothing could come of it other than a sexual harassment suit. She was his employee, even if she did report to Susan.

Dragging in a ragged breath, he watched her pace around the small porch. Something had her worked up. He shouldn't be concerned, because she wasn't his problem. Not unless it interfered with her job.

Tomorrow was another day. Maybe Jess would decide to leave and maybe she wouldn't. But it would be interesting to see how long this city girl lasted out here in the middle of nowhere.

Who was he trying to kid? He didn't want her gone.

****

Three weeks later, Jess leaned back in her office

chair and smiled. She was still here. All the backlog of work Hunter had piled in her office was now done. She'd created several new searchable databases, along with learning more about the ranch. Heck, she was even getting more comfortable around the animals. Well, all except the bulls. Those she still avoided at all costs.

"Hey, Jess," Susan said, striding into her office, all denim and cowgirl chic.

"What's up?" Susan's help had been invaluable over the last few weeks, along with being a buffer between her and Hunter. Thank goodness she'd been able to eat breakfast with Susan rather than Hunter.

"A truck load of cattle just pulled up."

"What?" Jess jumped out of her chair. "It's not due for another week." She grabbed the file from the holder on her desk. Would this snafu be her downfall? No. Her spine stiffened. While Hunter had been out on the ranch working with his men, she was aware of every time he was even close to her. He was always watching her, waiting for her to slip up.

"I think I'll leave this little problem in your hands," Susan said with an evil grin.

"Thanks so much." Jess grinned, taking the sting out of her words. She ran to the front door and sprinted outside where a large man climbed out of the cab of a semi-truck. "Hi, I'm Jess." She held out her hand.

"Ma'am." A full-bearded, tall man tipped back his cowboy hat and grinned down at her before grasping her hand while cracks and pops of the cooling metal emanated from the truck. "If you'd be so kind to tell me where I can unload, I can be out of your way quickly."

She'd grown to love the easy manners of ranch people. She hoped this man took her news well. "There's a slight problem."

"What's that, honey?" He frowned and shifted from one foot to the other.

She blew out a breath. Come on, she'd dealt with mix ups before. "This shipment wasn't due to arrive until next week."

Understanding dawned onto the man's ruddy face. "That's correct. The original date was next week, but it was changed."

"By who?"

He hooked his thumbs in his jeans pockets as through settling in for a long discussion. "Hunter. He asked for the shipment to arrive early."

"He did?" Jess's ire spiraled upwards. Hunter moved up a shipment without telling her? Was he testing her? Trying to see if she could handle it or not? Anger churned in her belly. These "little" changes unnerved her. Hunter threw every road block he could.

Why? Because he wanted her off his property. Out of a job. Tension gripped her shoulders like a vice. The sweaty, overworked driver in front of her didn't deserve her wrath, Hunter Knight did.

Forcing a polite tone so not to offend the man who was blameless in the matter, she said, "If you'll hold on for a few minutes, let me go find Mr. Knight to find out where he wants the cattle." Without waiting for the man to answer, she marched past him and toward the stable where Hunter was working.

Damn billionaire cowboy. Her irritation at him climbed higher as she quickened her steps. Jess stormed into the barn, past the horses to the end where she knew Hunter was working. She was about to call his name when she froze in place.

A shirtless Hunter stood next to one of the paint horses. He had a dandy brush in his hand, moving it over the horse's coat in a circular motion. Oh Lord. Sanity deserted her, leaving her exposed to his raw sex appeal and masculinity. Her breasts swelled and a familiar ache started between her thighs.

Her gaze caressed Hunter's shoulder flexing as he brushed the horse. When he turned she noticed the fine black hair covering his chest, and how it tapered down beneath his jeans.

Heat flamed inside her, fast and furious like a wildfire blazing out of control. She wanted to brush her fingertips over his well-defined chest, to caress his masculine nipples, to feel his body against hers as she gripped his butt, pulling him to her.

Jess closed her eyes against the image of the two of them naked, lying in the hay, and Hunter making...Jess drew in a sharp breath and opened her eyes. Lust had no place in her life, not now, maybe not ever. And not with a rodeo cowboy.

She counted to a hundred as she fought for control over her lust. Thank goodness, Hunter was oblivious to her presence.

"I need to talk to you." Her voice was strong and confident. Her reaction to him was physical, nothing more. Lack of sex, nothing she couldn't force out of her mind in exchange for sanity.

"What can I do for you?" His gaze didn't wander from his task.

"I'd like an explanation as to why you changed the date on the cattle shipment." She wasn't asking him. She wanted an answer. Demanded was more like it.

"Didn't I tell you?" He threw her a sexy grin, one that begged her to forgive him.

"Don't give me what you've been shoveling, Knight." She moved forward.

"Stop," he yelled.

Jess halted at the harness of his voice taking her by surprise. "What's wrong now?"

"You're not dressed to come in here." He gestured to her shoes.

"These are perfectly fine."

"Look down, Jess."

She did and grimaced. The area was not only wet, but hay clung to every surface. "I didn't wear boots because I didn't realize I'd have to track you down to deal with the early shipment."

"Can't do your job, sweetheart?" His tone was condescending as he led the horse into a clean stall before returning to her side.

"I can do my job, but it's your job to keep me informed when you make a change. This error is on your shoulders, cowboy."

Their gazes clashed and his eyes darkened. He marched over to her, his sexy body looming over her. She wouldn't back down, he was in the wrong.

"Have you forgotten who's in charge here?"

All she had to do was reach out and explore the angles of his face with her fingers. "No." She folded her arms across her chest. He took her breath away, but she was still in charge of her emotions. "But that doesn't mean I have to take the muck you're shoveling."

"Is it any wonder you were fired from your last job with that attitude?"

"I didn't get fired." Damn the man. She'd had enough of his crap. "For your information, I resigned from my last job." She jabbed him in the chest with her finger to punctuate her words.

"Is the pressure getting to you?" He threw her a wicked grin. "Because you know what to do." He shrugged. "Just walk away. Forget you ever came to work for me. Easy thing to do." His eyes glinted with the challenge, the corners of his mouth twitching.

"Ugh." She threw her hands up in the air. "What is it with you? Afraid of losing out to me in our agreement? Is that why you keep sabotaging me? Afraid of being beat by a woman?" From giving her a mountain of work, to making her seek him out for a little things, now to this. She'd had enough.

His eyes went from dark to fiery. A twinge of anxiety shot through her veins. She was very much aware they were here alone. Not that Hunter would hurt her, she was sure of that. But damned if he didn't provoke her and she wasn't so sure she wanted to have a confrontation now. Maybe it was time for a strategic retreat. Jess turned.

"Oh no you don't get to leave yet." The gruff words reached her ears as he snagged her around the waist and pulled her off her feet.

"Hunter," she yelled as he hoisted her into the air and began to walk. "This isn't—"

"Shut up." His tone was harsh.

The scowl on his face had her swallowing her words. It might be prudent to stay silent right now. While his stride was sharp and angry, his hands were gentle in the way they cradled her body. Heat and anger warred inside her, tying her emotions into knots.

The sun blinded her as they left the barn. "You can put me down."

He glared at her and kept walking until they were on the other side of the barn. Out of the sun. He set her on her feet, but his arms stayed around her waist.

Her hands rested on his bare shoulders. *Push him away.* But her fingers drifted down to his dark hair covered chest. His hair prickled her skin making her fingers tingle with excitement of exploring further. No man should ever feel this good.

"Hunter." His name caught in her throat as she glanced up at him. The scowl on his face was gone and replaced with something infinitely more dangerous, something she refused to put a name to.

"There's only one way to quiet a woman." He lowered his head and his lips captured hers.

CHAPTER FOUR

Jess sighed as Hunter's lips covered hers. She'd been afraid of this. The tension between them was pulled tight. His tongue traced the seam of her lips. If he demanded entrance to her mouth, she might have resisted, but his tenderness, his care was her undoing. Her lips parted.

His tongue invaded, tangling with hers as he deepened the kiss. Her arms slid up to his shoulders, to entwine themselves around his neck. Her heart pounded when his palms cupped her butt and pulled her close.

She closed her eyes. The scent of horses, sweat and masculinity penetrated her nose. She inhaled. Hunter's scent. All male. Tangy, woodsy, and spicy. Hunter broke the kiss. His hot breath caressed her cheeks, before moving to her eye lids.

A shiver swept up her spine as he kissed her closed eyes, then moved to her temple, before his lips made their way to the curve of her neck. He nibbled and licked at her skin. "You taste so sweet," he whispered against the base of her throat.

His hands slid up from her butt and tunneled under her shirt. The touch of his palm against her bare skin jolted her back to reality.

"Hunter, we can't." She forced her arms between them, pressing her palms against his chest.

"Of course we can." He started to tighten his hold.

"No." She pushed hard until his hands slipped from her body to his sides. Jess took a step back and took a deep breath. Her knees wobbled but held her upright. That would be all she needed to do, face plant in front of him after such a fantastic kiss.

Damn. What was she thinking. This was so not a good idea. None of it. She wanted to be angry with him, but she was angrier with herself. She never should have let it go so far.

She couldn't look at him. "I'm sorry," she whispered, before she spun around and fled. Jess ran until she reached her temporary home. Once there, she slammed the door behind her and leaned against it.

Her breath came in short, hard pants. How could she let him kiss her? Was a kiss worth her sanity? Her job? A chance at pulling her from the financial mess that had brought her to the Double K in the first place? Pushing away from the door, she made her way to the sofa and collapsed. She'd lost all control when his lips touched her, her fingers tangling in his dark hair, her hips wiggling against his. Hell, she'd been all but trying to have sex with him.

Shame washed over her. When had she lost control over her senses? Who was she kidding. The second he touched her all her senses were focused on one thing. Him. How quickly he'd destroyed her carefully built defenses.

The honking of a horn had her surging to her feet. The cattle. She took a deep breath, then let it out. Repeating the technique until she could push the kiss away into a small corner of her brain. She wouldn't be brought down by a cowboy. Not in this lifetime.

Jess jogged over to the truck five minutes later. "I'm so sorry for the delay." She smiled at the driver. "If you'll unload the cattle in the north paddock that would be appreciated." The area was empty, Hunter could move them if he wanted them elsewhere. She didn't care if he liked it or not.

"No problem, ma'am." He climbed into the cab of his truck. The engine rumbled to life, and he drove off.

****

Hunter leaned against the barn wall and cursed. What the hell was wrong with him? Grabbing Jess like that and kissing her? He hadn't been able to help himself, seeing her riled up and so damn beautiful killed all rational thought. He had no excuse. His behavior appalled him.

The sound of a semi had his head jerking to the right. The cattle delivery. Guilt ate at him at forgetting to tell Jess he'd changed the delivery date. Not to mess Jess up, but because his knee was healing fast and he wanted the ranch caught up before he went back to the rodeo circuit.

Pushing away from the wall, Hunter jogged over to the truck. At least Jess's mind was still working, she had directed the driver to the north pasture, just where he wanted them. He had to respect she'd learned enough to know what to do. He'd find Jess later. Right now there was work to be done.

****

"Where's Jess?" Hunter asked his sister four

hours later.

"In her office. Why?" His sister's light brown eyes narrowed.

"Thanks." He ignored her look and strode down the hall to Jess's office. He smelled of cattle and hay, but it couldn't be helped. He'd given her four hours to get over her upset about the cattle delivery and their kiss. It was only fair. Even city girls needed a chance to regroup.

Jess might be trouble on a stick, but he couldn't remember when he enjoyed a kiss so much. Her soft lips against his making him want to explore other parts of her body. The way her tongue tangled with his, the little mewing sounds she made when his fingers found bare skin so soft and sweet? It made him ache.

He stopped cold at her closed office. No one shut their doors here. He grasped the knob and turned it. Jess was at her desk, head bent over the papers on her desk, and she didn't even look up lost in concentration.

"Hey, Jess."

She jumped at the sound of his voice and he hid a smile. He'd surprised her. Good.

Her pert nose wrinkled. "Don't you believe in knocking, or are closed doors an anomaly to you?"

"We don't close our doors here." He sauntered over and leaned against her desk. Her hair was slipping out of its confinement, forehead creased as she concentrated.

"I needed some peace and quiet." She didn't even bother to look at him.

"Outside of me, and Susan, how many visitors have you had?"

She shook her head and continued to type. Hunter didn't like being ignored. He'd decided he needed to apologize for forgetting to tell her about him moving the cattle shipment up, but her attitude annoyed the hell out of him.

"I need your attention for a minute."

She sighed, then glared up at him. "Okay, boss. What is it?"

Her saucy tone and the mischief in her eyes prodded the bull. Without giving himself time to think about resisting the temptation, he pulled her out of her chair, his fingers ripping the tie from her hair.

"What the hell are you doing?"

"I like your hair down." Where was that wild untamed woman he'd held in his arms a few hours ago? The one who unleashed a current of fiery desire.

"I don't care what you like." She raised her arms to gather her hair back up.

"You did a few hours ago," he said capturing her wrists as her chestnut hair flowed over her shoulders.

"That was a mistake." Her voice was soft and her cheeks pink.

His instincts kicked in. Jess was fighting her attraction to him.

"My only mistake." He maneuvered her away from her chair and into his arms, "was letting you get away."

"Let me go, Hunter." Her body trembled and her sexy mouth parted on a shuddering breath.

Hunter frowned. What was wrong with this

picture? "I'm not going to hurt you." He would never hurt a woman. Ever. Had someone hurt her? The thought made his blood boil.

"This is not a good idea." She placed her palms against his shoulders and pushed.

"What..."

The phone rang and she sprang away from him. Jess reached over and snatched up the receiver.

"Double K Ranch, this is Jess, may I help you." She was ever the professional and he wondered how she turned her feeling off so fast.

Hunter leaned against the file cabinet. He'd let her take care of this call and then they'd get back to business. Personal business.

"I don't know how you got this number. Yes, I understand." Her voice was tight. All the color bleached from her lovely face. "But that isn't my signature."

Was there trouble? He took a step toward her but she held up her hand. He'd wait.

"Yeah, right. I've already made arrangements, that's all I can do. Please do not call here again." She slammed the receiver down, flopped down into her chair, and lowered her face into her hands.

His gut tightened. He didn't like this at all. Jess struck him as a woman who could handle anything that life threw at her. She was just as stubborn as he was. But right now she looked defeated. He didn't like it. "Jess, what was that all about?"

Her head snapped up, she squeezed her eyes shut, then opened them. "Nothing. It's personal." Her voice was devoid of any emotion.

Hunter pondered if he should press her for more information, but decided he'd wait until later. Right now he had another question burning in his gut.

"Why did you tell the driver to put the cattle in the north pasture?"

She gave him a wary look. "According to the records, the last time there were any cattle there was four months ago. It seemed like the logical choice." She plucked a rubber band from the jar on her desk and pulled her hair back. "From the reading I've done, you rotate the cattle every four to five months."

"You got that from reading the ranch records?" He didn't mean to sound so shocked, but most people wouldn't pick up how you had to let the land recover before putting animals back to graze just from reading some records.

"I may be a city girl, but I'm not stupid." She crossed her arms over her chest, leaned back in her chair, and stared at him. Defiant. Proud. A woman who wouldn't back down from a challenge.

"I never said you were." He enjoyed how she wouldn't take any crap from him. She wasn't afraid to put him in his place. Exhilaration filled his veins. He loved a spunky woman.

"Then quit treating me like I can't even add two and two."

"When have I done that?" He conceded that he did treat her slightly differently than he did his sister, but his sister had grown up on the ranch. He couldn't afford any screw ups, not with his stock, his ranch, or anything else in his life.

"You do it all the time." Her fingers flew over the

keyboard, pulling up the directory file. "You check almost every piece of work I do." She highlighted his initials next to the file.

Hunter cursed silently. He'd forgotten he'd made sure their files showed who accessed them last. "I am the boss." He leaned his hip against her desk, crossing his feet.

"That's your excuse for everything." She shook her head. "Did you inspect Chris's work this way? The previous office manager? Why are you obsessed with checking up on me?"

"Because you need a keeper. You have a pair of boots, yet you wear sneakers. You skip meals. And you're too damn sexy." Those last words slipped out before he could stop them.

Her spine stiffened and her features froze colder than a winter storm. "I'm sorry I wasn't born on some dirt patch out in the middle of no man's land with only a horse for company. I can't change where I was born and raised, but I can do this job. If you'll let me." She pushed back her chair.

"Where are you going?" He grasped her arm when she went to push by him.

"We could argue about this all night, but I'm not going to beat a dead horse. Besides, Susan asked me to dinner along with Chris." She shook off his hold and marched out of the room.

Excitement tingled under his skin as he allowed himself a smile. It had been a very long time since any woman, except his sister and mother stood up to him. And dang if this little spitfire didn't.

He rubbed his chin. He wasn't ready to be done

with her. A smile crept over his lips as he headed for his cabin. Since Jess was having dinner with Susan, he'd just have to invite himself. Because Jess made him hotter than a Texas summer heat wave, and he wouldn't mind if she singed him just a bit.

****

Jess smoothed her denim skirt as she stood on Susan's front porch and frowned at how her fingers trembled. Her nerves all revolved round that damn cowboy. Hunter made her feel more feminine than another other man ever had. He aroused a need in her she didn't want to have. And the kiss today? Forbidden, fabulous and straight out of her fantasies.

It scorched her straight to the ground. She'd fought against giving in to him, but she had, and while she'd like to regret it she couldn't. The man knew how to kiss. Even if it meant nothing to him. Just another tactic to scare her into leaving.

You'd think after a couple weeks, he'd realize she wasn't going anywhere. And she wasn't. She'd fought off advances of men before. Heck, she'd decked her last boss for hitting on her. Why hadn't she done that with Hunter?

Because she was attracted to him. Because she wanted him with a ferocity that scared her. Because he was off limits. His dark wavy hair begged for her to run her fingers through the silky stands. His lips asked for her to kiss him, his heat called out to her body, and her skin tingled from his slightest touch.

"So not fair," she whispered as she shook her head to dispel the images her thoughts invoked.

"What's not fair?"

The amused male voice caused her to jump. She spun around. As if she'd conjured him, Hunter stood on the bottom step, his damp hair curling at the ends and his chocolate eyes appraising her from head to toe. Desire curled in her belly, leaving her hot and achy in places best left alone.

"Nothing," she mumbled. Damn if the jeans he wore didn't hug every muscle he had, and he had a lot. And was that...she looked away from his fly.

"You look beautiful," he said, his voice soft, almost reverent.

"Thanks." She shifted from one foot to the other. Why was she acting like a sky school girl on her first date?

"Shall we?" He reached around her and opened the front door, then motioned for her to precede him.

"Hey, you two," Susan said when they walked in. Her friend didn't act surprised at seeing them together.

"Hi." Jess hurried to her friend's side to escape Hunter's tantalizing presence. When had a man ever affected her like this? Ned certainly hadn't. With Ned she'd been in control of her emotions.

What was the matter with her? He was a cowboy. She couldn't be attracted to him. It was all a game to Hunter, anyway. A game of control. Well, she controlled her life now, not some man. Even one who tormented her dreams.

She glanced up to find Hunter staring at her. His brown eyes filled with need. Hot waves of desire flowed through her. How the hell was she going to cope with him tonight? The suggestion hit her. Play the game. Hunter was flirting with her in an effort to make her leave. It was time to turn the tables.

He'd run for the hills before the night was over. Oh yes, two could play this game and Hunter was about to meet his match.

An hour later, Jess smiled as Hunter glared at her with suspicion in his eyes and confusion on his face. She'd played the flirting female all through dinner. Glancing over at Susan, Jess saw her struggling to keep the laughter from bursting out.

She hadn't had time to clue her friend into her plan. Yes, Susan recognized what she was doing from their time together in college. And Susan was enjoying every second of her brother's bewilderment. It wouldn't take much more to have Hunter on his knees.

"Why don't you and Jess go outside," Susan said. "Chris can help me clean up,"

"Sure." Hunter stood, then motioned for Jess to go ahead of him.

"Sounds good." Standing, she slid by Hunter. Once they were on the porch she glanced at him. He stood near the door like a cornered mountain lion ready to leap away at the first hint of trouble.

"It's hot tonight." Jess fanned herself with her hand watching him from beneath her lashes.

"Something is cooking all right." He pushed away from the house, strode to the railing and looked out.

"Maybe it's you, cowboy." She sidled up next to him and trailed her palm over his broad shoulders. He tensed.

"How much did you drink tonight?"

"Are you implying I'm drunk?" Let him think of her that way. Let him thing she was wild and untamed. Let him think she was everything he disliked. Maybe he'd keep his distance from her. She walked her fingers down his arm, each muscle in his arm tightened with each touch.

"Either you're drunk or aliens have taken over your mind." He stepped away from her.

Jess barely prevented a laugh from escaping. She was getting to him. "Not drunk, and no aliens, darlin'." She almost flinched at the sugary sweet tone of her voice. Hunter needed to be taught a lesson and she was the one to do it.

"Darlin'?" The confusion in his eyes turned to feral desire and stopped her in her tracks. "You can call me that as you writhe beneath me in my bed."

Flames of desire licked up her belly. Okay, maybe she'd gone a little too far with the endearment, but his outright puzzlement was worth it. His words shook her. Did her really want her? "Hunter." She reached her hand out to him.

His heated gaze remained focused on her. "What is with you tonight? What's your end game?"

"Me? You're the one who started this." Ah damn, she hadn't meant to blurt that out.

"Ahhhh...." He took her hand and tugged her to him.

Her breath caught in her throat as he held her in his embrace. His heat called to her, and she fought not to melt against his muscular chest. Inch by inch, he guided her closer. Oh Lord, she fought down the panic snaking around her body.

"I think the lady doesn't know when she's in trouble." His mouth was right above hers, his breath caressing her skin.

"What makes you think that?" Breathe. She inhaled. She barely prevented a moan of pleasure escaping her lips as his scent of wood, spice and masculinity filled her senses. Her insides melted.

"You're playing with fire," he warned.

"No, you are." Oh the hell with it. She brushed her lips over his. His eyes grew wide. He tasted like coffee and she wanted more. Entwining her arms around his neck, she tugged him down.

Her tongue darted out, tasting his lips. Tasting his spiciness. She put everything thing she had into the kiss, using her lips and tongue. Her fingers curled at the back of his neck, but he didn't respond. Fighting against the rejection, she kept her lips on his.

His lips didn't twitch, or move. His hands were at her waist and...the next thing she knew he'd set her away from him. His chocolate brown eyes unreadable. "Tell Susan I'm checking on the horses." His touch disappeared. "I'll see you tomorrow."

Jess glanced down not wanting to see the rejection in his gaze, even as satisfaction flooded her. Results achieved. The hard ridge pressing against his jeans spoke volumes. She'd given him a dose of his own medicine. But at what cost? Mortification hit her in the belly.

He jogged down the stairs, then stopped at the bottom and glanced back at her with humor in his eyes. "We'll continue the kiss when there isn't an audience." He marched away.

Jess let out a raspberry. Her body hummed with awareness from their kiss.

"I've never seen anything so funny in all my life," Susan said, joining Jess as they watched Hunter disappear. "Details, please."

"What details?" Jess let out a breath not quite sure she'd scored a victory or not.

"The gory ones. I know you. You only play games with men to get even, which means Hunter started it. Did he made a pass at you?"

"Yes." Jess rubbed her hear palms over her arms. "There's more to it than a simple pass."

"Really?" Susan grabbed her arm and led her over to two rocking chairs. "Sit and spill."

"What about Chris?" She sat and wondered where the other man had disappeared.

" For some reason, he went out the back door the second we finished loading the dishwasher." Susan took her seat. "Now about Hunter."

"He's your brother."

"So what? If you had a sexy, delicious brother I'd be after him in a hot minute."

Jess laughed, then sobered. "But I do have a brother."

Susan grinned, "Ben is a little young for me. I like them older and experienced. Now spill."

"Hunter doesn't want me here and is trying to scare me away by flirting with me." And dang if she didn't respond to his flirting.

"So you decided to give him a taste of his own medicine?"

"Yes, but somehow I think it backfired." He'd only looked confused about her flirting, obviously aroused, but not upset.

"I love my brother, but his past history with women isn't a good one."

"What do you mean?" Jess's curiosity was peaked. Maybe that was the cure to get the feel and taste of Hunter's lips against hers out of her mind.

"Do you remember when I came home from college, I wrote you about the woman Hunter was seeing?"

"Sort of." Jess thought back, but right now the only image in her mind was one stubborn cowboy.

"Hunter was dating Shana, the witch from hell."

"That good?" Sarcasm dripped from Jess's voice as she patted her friend's hand when Susan's fingers curled around the chair arm.

"I'm being polite. She gave all of us women a very bad name and rap."

"Your brother sounds like he has bad taste in women." She grimaced. Did his bad taste include her? Somehow he didn't strike her as a type of man who could be taken in by a pretty face, but what did she know? She'd been taken in by Ned.

"Hunter's taste is fine. He picked you."

Jess blushed. "He hasn't picked me for anything." He wanted her off his ranch, plain and simple. He figured flirting with her would make her run. She was stronger than that.

"He's attractive."

As hell, but Jess stayed silent. She wasn't about to admit to her best friend that her brother was sex on a stick. The last thing she wanted was Susan playing matchmaker because she would.

"Well," Susan continued to fill the silence. "Shana played Hunter. Hung around him like a buckle bunny."

"Buckle bunny?' Jess laughed as she pictured the Easter bunny with a belt and buckle around its furry body.

"Women who hang around the rodeos trying to pick up cowboys. Like groupies."

"I get the picture." It wasn't a pretty one either. She didn't remember her father ever saying anything about that. "So why did Hunter get involved with her?"

"On the surface, Shana was everything a guy could dream of. Beautiful, smart, and sweet. As long as she got her way. Inside, she was selfish, spoiled, and had a mean streak that could even scare the meanest bull back into its pen." Susan waved her hand. "I really think Hunter was lonely. He was on the circuit constantly, plus Mom and Dad were pressuring him to settle down and have a house full of kids."

"And Shana was more than ready to take the job."

"Yeah." Susan sighed. "She acted like friggin' Betty Crocker and Dale Evans wrapped up into a neat little package. She had us all fooled."

"Somehow I don't see Hunter falling for a woman like that."

"He did. Hunter is one of the most well known bull riders on the circuit, but not only that, his training methods with horses has everyone demanding his time. How he came to marry Shana when all she wanted was his money and the prestige of the Knight name, I'll never know."

"Married?" Jess hadn't been prepared for that. If he was married, then why was he flirting with her? Was she wrong about him? Was he as faithless as Ned?

"Not now. He divorced her a year later. Thank God."

Divorced. Jess's heart began beating again. Thank goodness, Hunter wasn't the type of man to cheat on a woman. He was honest and above board with her in all aspects. Then something else dawned onto her. "Let me guess, Shana wasn't from around here." She blew out a breath. Well, that would explain Hunter's objections to her, even his open hostility, but his methods sent mixed signals.

"You got it. A city gal, through and through. Shana didn't like the ranch or when Hunter went on the circuit. But she liked his money, especially when his net worth became public."

"The ranch is his business. He's a rodeo cowboy at heart. He's not going to give that up." While Jess may not like bulls, she appreciated the ranch as a successful family business. Her reasons for dreading the rodeo were different from Shana's.

"Shana didn't see it that way. She wanted to throw elaborate parties whenever she wanted to and expected Hunter to be there. She didn't care if the cattle needed to be moved, if a horse was in labor, or if he had a championship ride coming up. All she cared about was herself and money."

"Coldhearted bitch." She hated that Hunter

lumped her in with his ex-wife as the same kind of woman. A fierce protectiveness for Hunter seized Jess' heart. He didn't need her protection, but Shana had played with his heart when all she'd wanted was his money.

"Good summation." She touched Jess's forearm. "I love Hunter, but he can be bullheaded at times."

"Now I see how his ex gave us city women a bad name." Did she remind him of his ex? Did he think she was here to trap him into marriage? Because he was mistaken. The last thing on her mind was marriage. And marrying a cowboy? Out of the question. "How do I make him understand I can do this job?"

"Hunter hates to lose and he's going to use every trick in the book, fair or foul to win the bet. It's up to you to show him he can't run you off."

"Great advice, but how do I do that?" Jess surged to her feet and walked over to the porch railing. She hated being at a loss on how to fix something.

"Keep him on his toes. Just keep doing what you've been doing." Susan joined her. "Show him you can do the job; educate him that not all city women are like his ex."

"I can handle anything he throws at me." Her reaction to his flirting told her otherwise. Why couldn't she be as unaffected as he was?

"He's attracted to you."

Jess's head swiveled in surprise. "Your brother just wants a quick roll in the hay."

"Really?" Susan leaned her hip on the railing and crossed her arms over her chest. "If that was true, he could go into Dallas and find a woman. The wattage the two of you put out when you're together could light up this ranch for an entire year."

"Susan." Jess covered her hot face with her hands.

Susan tugged at her wrists. "I love my brother, and I love you like a sister."

Tenderness filled Jess's heart at Susan's words.

"Here's the thing." Susan released her hold on Jess' wrists. "You play the brazen woman as a defense mechanism. I saw it enough in college to recognize it. But Hunter doesn't know that. He's going to believe what he sees. The party girl. So be careful."

Tears sprang to Jess's eyes. Susan saw so much, more than she realized. And never asked why Jess needed a job or why she came to Texas. She loved Susan all the more for it. "Thanks. You are a true friend." She pulled Susan into a hug.

"I am. When you're ready to talk, I'll be here." Susan stepped out of the embrace. "Don't let my brother get the best of you."

"I won't." Jess bounced down the stairs and strode toward her home. She had some thinking to do.

****

The next morning, Hunter was putting Liberty through her paces in the arena. She would make a wonderful barrel horse. The sun glinted off the horse's coat reminding him of Jess's chestnut hair.

Jess. The annoying, sexy, sensual woman filled his mind. He'd tossed and turned last night trying to figure out what she was trying to accomplish by flirting with him. He was still sporting a partial erection from her banter.

He deserved her teasing, but it didn't stop his body from reacting. Plus, he wondered just how far her teasing would go.

Liberty's ears perked up. Hunter glanced around to find the object of his thoughts striding toward the arena and him like a woman on a mission.

"Hey, Hunter." Her cheery voice carried over the hard-packed earth to his ears.

"Morning." He gave Liberty a pat, dismounted, and sauntered over to the fence where she stood. "What brings you out here?"

She looked fresh and well rested. Part of him was irritated she wasn't losing any sleep over him.

"Mr. Willows called. Something about breeding his mare."

"Okay." Bart wanted to breed his mare with Thunder, Hunter's stallion. "What did he say?"

"He'd be here this afternoon around one."

"Fine." At least Thunder would have some fun and relieve some sexual tension. Hunter wished he could do the same. He could, but he only wanted one woman in his bed right now and she was standing in front of him.

She hesitated, mumbling something beneath her breath. "That's it." She turned away.

He reached out, grasped her by the shoulder and spun her to face him. "What's your hurry?"

Jess stiffened at his touch and that was okay. Even if she reacted in ways he didn't expect, he needed to keep up with his teasing.

"I have work to do." Surprise glinted in her eyes

as she took a step back. He followed her gaze over his shoulder.

"Liberty." He let out a laugh. The horse's nose was practically resting on his shoulder. "I should introduce you two. This is Liberty." Hunter turned to allow the horse to move closer. Liberty moved right up to the fence and Jess.

"That's nice." She shook off his hold.

"Come say hello." He stared at Jess. Her amber eyes were clouded with alarm and sweat glistened on her forehead.

"That's okay." She stumbled back a few feet.

"Jess." He jumped over the fence as she swayed on her feet. His hands closed over her upper arms. "You skipped breakfast again." What other explanation could there be? Susan had assured him, Jess was either eating with her or getting a full breakfast from Paddy, but her pale features told him otherwise.

He slipped his hands to her waist and frowned. Had she lost weight? Protectiveness welled up in him. If the woman wouldn't take care of herself, he'd do it for her.

"I didn't." The words were spoken between clenched teeth.

"Are you sick?" His fingers trailed over her forehead, sliding to her pale cheek, before gliding to where her pulse beat rapidly in her neck. Something wasn't right. Her pulse rate rivaled a jack hammer. Hunter studied her face. What was it? Fear? Was she afraid of him?

"I'm not sick." Her voice had strength in it now.

She blinked several times. "Why are you holding me?"

"Because if I don't, you'll pass out."

She shook off his hands and stepped away from him. "Don't be ridiculous."

Hunter crossed his arms over his chest and stared at her, unconvinced. "So let me get this straight. You didn't skip breakfast, you're not sick, and you're not going to faint."

"That's right." Her chin tilted up.

A slow grin tugged at his lips. "So it must be my overpowering presence."

Color rose to her cheeks before she said, "Go sit on a pile of cow dung."

"Only if you come with me." Before she could march away, he snagged her around the waist and pulled her into his embrace. Her breasts pressed against his chest, their hips aligning. Heaven. He was in heaven and hell. Passion and need filled him.

"Let me go." She squirmed in his arms.

"I might." He gazed into her eyes. A fire of need and desire burned in the depths of her amber eyes. While his protective instincts were still in high gear, he wanted to tap the passion he saw in her. He spread his fingers along her lower back and bent his head. His hat shifted and fell to the ground.

His lips found the pulse in her neck, and she jumped within his embrace. Her skin warmed under his lips. Hunter nuzzled his way to her ear, then ran his tongue around its shell. Soft and sweet. A shudder shook her frame, and her soft gasp encouraged him to continue. But he wanted more.

"Put your arms around me," he ordered his voice muffled by her skin. He ached to feel her embrace.

"Go to hell." Her voice husky with passion.

"I'm already there, *darlin'*." He bit down on her lobe. She wouldn't make things easy for him.

"Arrg."

Her growl of frustration reached his ears seconds before her hands tangled in his hair. Oh yes, that was what he wanted. Her hands on him, caressing him, holding him...pain.

"Ouch," he said.

Her fingers curled further into his scalp, pulling. "Let go, woman."

"Back off."

What choice did he have? He dropped his arms as he gave Jess some space.

"Thank you." She withdrew her hands from his hair.

Hunter reached up and massaged his scalp. Damn. This woman had one hell of a grip. He glanced at her. Her face was tight with tensions. "You're one tough filly," he muttered.

"I'm not one of your horses. I'm a person." She glared at him.

"You're a hell of an attractive woman."

"And you're impossible."

"But loveable." He chuckled at the expression of outrage on her face. She was so adorable when she was riled up. He did wonder where the flirtatious woman of last night had gone. Jess was blowing hot and cold, and for some reason he didn't mind it.

"Go back to your cows, cowboy."

"I expect you at barn number four at one this afternoon." Back to business for now.

"Whatever for?"

He didn't miss the exasperation in her tone. "Because I'm the boss." He wanted her out on the ranch today. "You need to learn all aspects of ranch life."

"My job is handling the office, not the livestock."

"Partially." He leaned down and picked up his hat. "You will be explaining our process to your clients. In order to do that, you need to observe how we breed a mare."

CHAPTER FIVE

Hunter's laughter followed Jess as she strode away from the arena. He kept pushing and pushing, trying to get her to leave. Her fingers curled into her palms, nails biting into the soft flesh. Well, she wasn't a quitter and she wasn't about to let this sexy cowboy get the best of her. No way, no how. He didn't have anything to lose. She did.

She cringe at her lacked the willpower to push him away when he drew her into his embrace. With each steamy touch and lusty glance, sexual innuendoes nibbled away at her defenses. Her mouth said one thing but her body followed his sensual demands.

His strong arms around her made her bones melt, and gave her pause. He made her so aware of the sensual woman she kept hidden. That side of her caused nothing but trouble, yet he was able to draw it out easily. She wanted him.

What? Jess stopped in her tracks. Oh God, she wanted Hunter. A cowboy. Lust surged through her veins. No, lust made you weak. It was better to keep her feelings hidden. Forget how welcoming his arms were. Forget how gentle and protective he was. Forget that Ned had never made her feel that way.

Ned. Ned was the reason she was in this mess to begin with. Ned caused all her heartache in the first place. She was smarter now. She wouldn't allow lust to override her good judgment as she'd done with Ned. If she gave into Hunter, she'd lose her job.

Men, who needed them? She didn't. She wouldn't let lust rule her life. No matter how satisfied Hunter could make her, she wouldn't let him interfere with her job or her life. Jess smiled. Men, like fine wine, were better off left alone until they matured.

Right now it was time to get her work done. Back in her office, she grabbed two books off the shelf and sat down. Time for a primer on horse breeding. That way, there wouldn't be any surprises. She opened the first book and began reading.

Watch out, Hunter Knight, I'm coming, fully loaded.

Five minutes before one, Jess found herself outside barn number four. Hunter and three of the ranch hands were waiting. Next to Hunter was an impossibly large horse. The horse snorted and moved restlessly.

Mr. Willows had arrived thirty minutes ago with is horse, but the horse next to Hunter was a stallion, not a filly.

"Go get Lady Pride," Hunter said to his men.

"Afternoon, Jess," said Cal, another ranch hand, as he passed her.

"Afternoon." She acknowledged the men.

"About time you got here," Hunter said.

"I'm early." She glanced down at her watch.

"Things went faster than we anticipated."

"Okay." She kept her distance from both Hunter and the horse.

"This is Thunder." He reached up and patted the horse's head.

"Nice." Her stomach somersaulted. She swallowed hard and prayed she could get through this. She knew what to expect from her reading, but she didn't expect the horse to be so large.

"Thunder is part Thoroughbred, part Arabian. He's a first class horse." He ran his hands over the flank of the horse, keeping him calm. Thunder snorted and raised his head.

Cal and the other men led the mare into the small fenced paddock. The mare's eyes were wide. Jess's heart constricted. The poor mare looked frightened.

Her attention was taken from the mare to Thunder as he snorted and pawed the ground.

"Easy boy." Hunter crooned to the horse, leading him in a tight circle. He continued to talk to the stallion keeping him calm.

She turned her gaze back to the mare. Her tail had already been wrapped, and now they were putting hobbles on her to keep her from kicking Thunder. As the men moved the mare into position, Hunter walked Thunder into the area. Cal met him and took the reins.

Hunter slipped out of the paddock and came up behind her. His chest pressed lightly against her back, as he stretched his arms around her, until he grasped the fence in front of them. His heat surrounded her. She did her best to ignore him and concentrate on the horses.

"So now what?" she asked, trying to control her breathing at his nearness.

"First, we'll let the two tease each other. Horsey

foreplay," he whispered close to her ear.

She nodded but kept her eyes on the horses, trying to ignore Hunter's warmth seeping into her bones. The mare squealed as the stallion passed by. Thunder nipped at the mare's neck.

"Look at Lady's tail." Hunter's warm breath stirred her hair. "See how she's raising it. She's letting Thunder know she's ready for him."

"A raised tail is only one sign." Jess tried to focus on the horses rather than Hunter's presence behind her. She reached out and gripped the fence.

"True." He placed his hands over hers. "See how she reacts to him. Her squeals mean she's ready. The sight and smell of Lady have Thunder going off the deep end. It's just like a woman trying to drive a male crazy."

The air around them sizzled. Jess shifted from one foot to the other. How could an act of nature arouse her? Her breathing grew shallow as Thunder stomped his hooves before reared up over the mare. She gasped when she got a look at this well-endowed male animal.

"Oh God." Jess lowered her eyes. "He's going to kill her."

"No, he won't." Hunter leaned closer. "Look at them."

She responded to the command in Hunter's voice. Her head rose and her gaze zeroed in on the horses. Her pulse quickened. She shouldn't be watching the horses mate. It wasn't natural. She wasn't a voyeur by nature, but she couldn't stop staring. And if she did turn away, Hunter would win, and she couldn't let that happen.

"Does Lady look in pain to you?" he asked.

She swallowed. "No," she whispered. It was true, Lady's eyes were glazed over in what Jess wanted to believe was ecstasy. The mare stood still as Thunder thrust into her. And with each thrust, Lady pushed back and craned her neck toward the stallion.

Heat flooded Jess' veins. Her core throbbed, pulsing outwards until she was sure her body vibrated with need. The horses continued their mating, and her breathing grew short and choppy.

Did Hunter move closer? It seemed as if his chest was pressing harder into her back. She forced herself to keep watching the horses. She couldn't look away, she couldn't back down. She had to remain passive and ignore the moisture gathering between her thighs.

The horses shrieked and Jess shivered. Thunder thrust in and out of Lady at will. The men stood around the pair, encouraging Thunder. They weren't crude or leering, but supportive and helpful.

Lady screamed as Thunder plunged into her. It was pleasure, Jess saw it in the way the mare reacted to the stallion. Lady wasn't trying to escape, but wanted to get closer to Thunder.

Was this what making love with Hunter be like? Was it suppose to be like this? A total loss of control? A shudder coursed through her body. Her fingers were pried off the fence and enfolded into hot skin. Her fingers tightened around Hunter's as she continued to watch the horses.

Thunder let out a cry and the horse stiffened over the back of the mare. Jess's knees went weak. If

Hunter hadn't stood so close behind her she would have fallen to the ground.

His arms encircled her waist and he walked them backwards until they were out of sight of the paddock. Coolness hit her skin as Hunter tugged her into a windowless tack room, his touch gentle as he turned her to face him.

There was color in her cheeks, but her eyes were wide and wildness danced in them. Her lower lip trembled. Unable to help himself, Hunter lowered his head and captured her mouth.

She opened to him like flower petals opening to the morning sun. His tongue plunged into her mouth. His hands slid from her arms, to her hair. He found the pins confining her hair and pulled them loose, letting them clatter to the floor. Wild silk tumbled over his skin.

Never before had a breeding affected him this way. It was because of Jess. She affected him in every sense of the word. He figured she'd come to the breeding and flirt with him. Instead, she was silent and reserved.

He tore his lips away from hers, pulling in a deep breath before nibbling his way to her ear, then down her neck.

Her own gasp for air spurred him on. His hands left the silky mass cascading around her shoulders, around to her front. His fingers grazed her breasts and she moaned.

Hunter slipped his hands to the waistband of her jeans. Within seconds her shirt was untucked and his fingers skimmed over hot, feminine skin. Slipping his hand up her spine, he found her bra. Within seconds it was unfastened and his palms covered her breasts.

"Oh my God, your hands feel so good," she whispered in his ear before she buried her face in his neck. Gone was the brazen hussy and in her place was the real Jess. The real woman.

He tweaked her nipples, causing them to stand at attention. He wanted to see if she tasted as sweet as she was soft. Putting some distance between their bodies, he pulled the shirt up and over her head, before tossing it aside. Her bra followed seconds later.

The sight of her plump, round breasts and pink nipples almost had him dropping to his knees. Instead, he lowered his head and ran his tongue over one engorged peak. Her fingers tangled in his hair.

Hunter stiffened, expecting pain, but this time she pulled him closer. He paid homage to one breast while his free hand played with the other. Her skin was soft and silky, just like a newborn foal's coat.

Fingers tugged at his hair. He released her nipple and gazed up at her. Passion filled her amber eyes gazing down at him. "You are so beautiful," he whispered.

She blushed. Her heart pounded against his palms. "I want to touch you."

"Be my guest." Oh yes, he wanted her hands all over him.

Her fingers fumbled with the buttons of his shirt. Hunter fought his impatience. As much as he wanted her to hurry, he wouldn't rush her. He wanted their lovemaking to be slow and sweet. To discover each other's hot zones.

His shirt inched up before it was pushed over his head. His stomach clenched as she ran her nails from his waist to his chest. Her touch was torture A most exquisite kind of torture.

When her fingertips slid over his nipples, his hands tightened on her waist. She gazed at him from beneath her lashes before she lowered her head. Hot, burning heat flamed over his skin as she ran her tongue around one flat disk and moved to the other.

His erection strained against the denim. He pushed Jess back up against the wall, pinning her with his body. He rotated his hips, letting her feel what she did to him.

Her moan of need almost pushed him over the edge. He captured her lips while his fingers fumbled with the snap on her jeans. He took a step back so he could lower them. His feet tangled in something, and at the last second he released his hold on her as he landed on his butt on the floor.

Jess gazed down at Hunter lying at her feet, her bra twisted around his boots. Mortification hit her like a runaway horse. What the hell were they doing? What was she doing? Oh, God. She leaned down and grabbed her shirt off the floor.

This shouldn't have happened. Never in a million years. Her hands shook as she tried to put her shirt on, she had to cover herself.

"Jess." His voice flowed over her like honey.

"Get dressed, cowboy." How could he just lay there and stare at her with those big brown eyes?

"Come on, Jess." His fingers caressed her calf just above her boots.

"Look cowboy, I'm not a cheap roll in the hay." She shoved her blouse into her jeans. She really should put on her bra. Sweet heaven, her faced flamed. It was still tangled around Hunter's feet. What had she been thinking? That was part of the problem, she wasn't thinking, but feeling. Allowing those crazy emotions to take over her once rational mind.

"Now, wait a darn minute." He tried to scrambled to his feet but her bra hampered his efforts.

"No." Keeping her back to the wall, Jess scooted past Hunter and out the door. The sunshine was cool against her overheated skin. Without thinking about it, she hightailed it to her house. Once there she slammed the lock home and flung herself across the bed.

Oh God, what had she done? She'd made out with Hunter before, but that didn't faze her as much as how they started undressing each other. If he hadn't fallen... She didn't want to think about that or his delicious sun-kissed skin. Shameful tears filled her eyes and slipped down her cheeks. How was she going to face him?

****

Hunter sat on the tack room floor, getting his erratic breathing under control as he stared at the closed tack room door wondering what the hell just happened. One second Jess had been hot and heavy for him, and the next she was running like a frightened virgin. Damn it. He had a boner the size of Texas and she'd run out on him. Frustration roared through his body, and outside of taking himself in hand there wasn't much he could do about it.

Taking a deep breath, he reached down and

removed her bra from where it tangled around his feet and stood up.

Picking up his shirt, he slipped it back on and tucked her bra into his jeans pocket. No sense in leaving evidence of his folly lying around. He strode to the door and stood there, willing his erection to go away.

Wasn't happening. His men would take care of the horses. Hunter opened the door, and then stomped across the hard packed ground toward his home. Why had Jess fled? From her moans and groans, she'd been into their lovemaking as much as he had.

His sex twitched in his jeans. Yeah, he was ready to explode and having her dash off irked him more than he wanted to admit. Once inside his home, he stomped down the hallway into his bedroom. A cold shower would help his libido, but it wasn't going to do anything for the memory of Jess's soft breasts burned into his brain.

He'd find a way to tame his wild filly, because he wasn't going to let a city girl have the upper hand.

****

Jess sighed, kicked the covers off, and got up. She couldn't sleep. What was the point of trying? Every time she closed her eyes all she saw was Hunter. The passion in his face, the desire in his eyes, and the softness of his touch.

With a sigh, she stepped outside into the cool night air. Thank goodness, when she had returned to the office Hunter hadn't been there and Susan had left her a note she was out showing a client around.

Jess hadn't expected to be so aroused by the sight

of the horses breeding. Reading about it made it sound all clinical and not interesting at all, but seeing it made a difference. Then there was her reaction to Hunter.

Even sleeping with Ned had never made her feel as alive, as excited, as sensual, as she did right now. Sex with Ned had been just that, sex. No foreplay, no cuddling. Hunter was very touchy feely and she craved it. Jess leaned against the wall.

How had she let Hunter drag her into the tack room? Okay, so maybe he didn't drag her, but... But what? Who was she kidding. Hunter hadn't forced her to do anything she didn't want to do. Time to admit it.

After Ned, she had wanted to believe she could never want another man, but Hunter soothed her aches and made her want more of his brand of loving. Oh Lord, she was in trouble. Big trouble. Trouble that started with a H and ended with an R. She flopped down onto the porch swing and stared out into the dark Texas night.

She still had six weeks left in her bet with Hunter. So that meant finding a way to deal with this attraction that didn't jeopardize her job. She wished he had as much at stake as she did. Setting the swing in motion, she wondered what he was doing. Probably sleeping. This was nothing but a game to him.

"Son of a..." The curse reached her ears over the chirping crickets.

Ah, so he couldn't sleep either. The evil side of her was gleeful. He was the one who'd kissed her senseless so he deserved to lose some sleep over it. Just then lights flared near the patio. A loud splash echoed in the night.

Rotten cowboy. He could work off his excess energy in the pool. The best way she knew to work off her feelings was to run, and it wasn't like she could get dressed and run. Well she could, but there was no telling what kind of trouble she'd find. Human or otherwise.

She laid her head back and closed her eyes. The image of Hunter rose in her mind, his strong arms pulling him through the water. What would he do if she walked over and joined him?

The two of them naked in the water flashed behind her closed eyelids before she snapped her eyes open. Heat gathered in her belly and flared. Her breasts were heavy. Damn it, the man could arouse her without even being close to her.

Her lips parted and a soft sound emerged. No. She shook her head and jumped to her feet. She wouldn't give in to this temporary lust. She didn't need a man.

With renewed determination she turned and strode back into the house. Want and lust didn't have a place in her life. Not right now, and certainly not with a rodeo cowboy. She'd do well to remember that.

****

The next morning, Jess sat at her desk and blew out a breath as she talked on the phone. "But I've been in Texas for the last few weeks, there is no way I signed anything," she muttered. Not the way she wanted to start out her day.

Movement caught her eye. She glanced up to see Susan standing in the door way. She motioned for her to enter.

"Yeah, well your information is wrong." How was it these creditors could find a phone number for her in Texas, but couldn't believe some signature on a loan in California wasn't hers. The pencil she had in her fingers snapped as the guy on the phone threatened to sue her. "Good luck with that." The receiver hit the cradle with such force the phone slid an inch.

"It's never going to end. I'm never going to be free of debt or Ned." Jess lowered her face into her hands. She might as well give up and declare bankruptcy. At least that would get the creditors off her back. But it wouldn't solve the problem of Ned forging her name on documents. "I'm sorry, Susan. It's just, my life is one big mess upon mess."

"What has Ned done?" The chair in front of her desk squeaked when Susan sat down.

"I was so friggin' stupid." Jess lowered her hands and stared at her friend.

"We all are at one time or another. Want to tell me about it?"

"Not really. All I really want to do is crawl in a hole and never come out." Burying her head in the sand was what got her into this mess in the first place. But right now, she didn't want to face any of it. Not Ned, not Hunter, not her own emotions.

"You obviously need to talk this out, so one of these days you and I will discuss it." The concern in Susan's features was still there as she leaned forward. "I came in here to ask you if you wanted to come to the dance tonight."

"Dance?" While a room of happy people didn't seem like a good way to get her life back together, maybe she could stand to blow off some steam.

"Just a local one. I did mention it on Monday."

"It slipped my mind." Lord, was it Friday already?

"It's just what you need." Susan's eyes danced with mischief. "You can kick back a few beers, get tipsy, and flirt with every cowboy in the place."

Why not go out? She could enjoy a beer or two, dance a little, let her hair down so to speak. "No flirting."

"Okay no flirting, but you need to get out and enjoy life a bit."

"This issue with Ned isn't going to go away."

"No, but for one night you need to relax and forget all your troubles."

Jess sighed. Susan was right. One night wasn't going to kill her. "Okay. Just promise me you won't let me go home with any strange men." Jess grinned at her friend to show she was joking. No amount of alcohol in the world would make her do that. She'd grown up and there was the little matter of her obsession with Hunter. No other man could compete.

"Promise." Susan put her hand on her heart with a big smile on her face. "You can dance with every Y chromosome in the place, just no going home with someone you don't know."

"Deal." The two laughed and Jess's mood lightened. A night out would do her a world of good.

CHAPTER SIX

"Remind me again how I let you talk me into this?" Jess said to Susan. They stood inside an old refurbished barn with country music wailing in the background. Fresh hay, spread over the plank flooring, gave the place a pleasant aroma. Dim lighting showed lots of cowboy hats in the crowd.

"Because you need it." Susan glanced over at Chris, who had accompanied them. "Would you get the beer? We'll snag a table." After Chris nodded, Susan grasped Jess's hand and yanked her through the teeming crowd until they found an empty table.

"What's your rush?"

"This is a good table. I didn't want someone else to grab it." Susan plopped on one of the chairs.

Jess shook her head as she pulled out the wooden chair and sat. Her fingers danced on the table top in time with the music.

"Beer?"

"Oh yes." Susan looked up at the woman. "Hi Becky, I didn't realize you'd be waiting on tables tonight."

"Just to get everyone started." She set down two beers. "And I'm only allowed to give you one glass. Anything more you have to get up and get yourself."

"Okay, Chris is getting us a pitcher."

"Then you're all set, see you later."

"Here, drink up." Susan pushed over a mug full of amber liquid topped by white foam.

Jess shook her head at her friend before picking up the glass and taking a sip. The head tickled her nose, and she licked her lips in case she had foam-lip. "Not bad."

"Not bad?" Susan shot her a puzzled look. "You used to down beer like water back in college."

"Things have changed."

Before Susan responded, one of the cowboy's approached. "Hi, Susan. Ma'am." He tipped his hat at Jess then returned his attention to Susan. The thirty-something man dressed like all the other men in the room. Long sleeved shirt, jeans, boots and the requisite cowboy hat.

"Hey, Ralph. This is my friend, Jess Sinclair." Susan turned to her. "Jess, Ralph Waters. He owns the Lazy W."

"It's nice to meet you, Mr. Waters. I believe you own the horses Lady J and Winter's Dream."

"Yes, I do. Please call me Ralph." He lifted his hat. "Would you like to dance?"

Jess opened her mouth to refuse when Susan spoke up. "Of course she would." Susan nudged her with her foot.

"Yes, I would." She plastered a big smile on her face and placed her hand into Ralph's.

"Have fun," Susan said with a wave as Ralph led her away from the table. Jess stared over her shoulder at her friend. What was Susan up to?

****

Hunter smiled and greeted people as he walked

into the dance hall. Well, maybe not a dance hall since it was an old converted barn, but still it was a place where they could all meet on Friday nights and let loose.

The music thrummed through his veins. He spotted Susan and Chris out on the dance floor. Did Jess come with them? He'd stopped by her place to ask her if she wanted to go, but there'd been no answer.

He shrugged away his tension. Tonight was a night for fun, to unwind, and get rid of the crap from the last month.

"Let's dance." Margie Waters grabbed Hunter by the arm, before he could find Jess, and pulled him out onto the dance floor.

Margie was Ralph's baby sister, and Ralph was a good client. Margie turned eighteen two weeks ago and Hunter suspected she was trying to see how far she could go before her brother reined her in. While she was too young for him, he didn't mind dancing with her.

"Where ya' been hiding yourself, Hunter?" Margie slid her arms around his neck, moving in time with the beat.

"Just working hard." Hunter swayed with the music, but kept a respectable distance between their bodies. No sense in giving Margie the wrong impression. There only one woman he wanted pressed against his body.

"Ralph said you had a new office manager."

"Yep." Hunter scanned the other couples on the floor, nodding to the men and smiling at the women.

"Ralph said she was very pretty." Her pink lips turned into a rebellious pout.

"What?" His gaze was about to return to Margie when he saw Jess in the arms of Ralph. Unbound jealousy coursed through him as he stared at the couple as they circled the room. Jess looked delicious in her white lace blouse, short denim skirt, and red cowboy boots. His body hardened.

"Who ya' scowling at?" Margie turned her head. "She's the office manager, isn't she?" Margie said, following his gaze.

He spun Maggie out and tugged her back before answering. "Yes" Hunter forced a smile and returned his attention to Margie.

Jess was turning him inside out. Ever since the day of the breeding, she wouldn't come near him. If he walked into the office, she'd slip out the back door. When she hadn't shown up for dinner at Susan's, he'd intended going to go get her until Susan informed him Jess was cooking her own meals for a few days. His sister's eyes danced with amusement when he commented that Jess didn't need to cook.

He'd figured with Jess trying to avoid him, she'd refuse to attend the dance. Just when he thought he had this woman figured out, she did the unexpected. And she went from zero to angry in less time than it took to get bucked off a bull. If he wanted her in his bed, he needed to practice some finesse when it came to Jess. She might be a party girl, but she had standards and he'd do well to remember the fact. Plus he was no longer sure about that party girl past.

But he needed to get her away from Ralph. Not

because Ralph wasn't a nice man. He was. He didn't want Jess getting too close to any of the local men. No sense letting her leave a trail of broken hearts when she left. He began to dance Margie closer to the couple.

The closer Jess came to him, the more his blood thrummed in his veins. Ralph held Jess closer than a saxophone player held his instrument. A possessive streak gripped him. He didn't believe in sharing and he wasn't about to share Jess with another male. Forget wanting to protect the men from broken hearts. That's not what he cared about. Jess was his. Not Ralph's, not anyone else's. His.

Cool it, cowboy. A tiny voice of reason, sounding a lot like one hot and spicy city woman he lusted after, penetrated the haze blurring his vision. How would it look if he rushed over and decked Ralph? The town would have a field day if he acted out of character. He needed to be cool about this.

"Hunter?" Margie's voice was soft.

"Sorry." He'd stopped dancing. Picking up the beat again, he swung Margie around. If he went off the deep end, all he'd manage to do is inflame Jess's temper. While he didn't mind getting burned, he'd rather it happened in private.

Forcing his gaze away from the couple, he smiled at Margie, determined to enjoy the dance with her, to save a little pride from what his friend's kid sister had observed. There would be time enough tonight to capture Jess.

****

Jess stiffened in Ralph's arms when she noticed

Hunter. She'd hoped he would stay home since Susan hadn't mentioned him. Damn her rotten luck.

"Dang, sorry," Jess mumbled as she stepped on Ralph's toe.

"It's okay." Ralph smiled at her, his tone polite.

Why couldn't she be attracted to him? Ralph seemed like a hard working, steady, nice cowboy. Nice. That was the problem. Ned had been nice and look how that had turned out. Nice didn't mean faithful. Nice didn't mean commitment. Nice didn't mean honest.

"What the hell is Margie doing?" Ralph asked, his grip tightening around Jess.

"Who's Margie?"

"My baby sister. She's dancing with Hunter."

Jess craned her neck to get a better look at Hunter with the cute, perky blonde who was draped all over him. Fickle cowboy. "I thought you liked Hunter?"

"I do. It's just that since my baby sister turned eighteen, she's been stringing some of the boys along. Dancing with Hunter might just rile up some of the local boys."

Eighteen? "Why is that?" Jess tilted her head. Did Hunter have qualms about breaking this young woman's heart? He better.

"Because Hunter is a hero around these parts. The boys look up to him. They all want to be like him."

"Hero worship?" She gave Ralph a tight smile.

"Yeah. Hunter's a good guy." He spun her around as he continued to talk. "He never plays with local girls because when you play with local girls, you pay the price."

"So why are you worried?"

"Not worried about Hunter at all, worried by baby sister will think Hunter's kindness means more than it does."

"Is that right?" Jess tried to wrap her mind around the small town ideals. So did that mean she was fair game?

"Yep." He spun her again. "We're a very tight knit community. We care about our young people."

"But to interfere with their love life? The experimentation that comes with being a young person?"

"More like guidance. If Hunter had listened to some of the town folks about Shana, he never would've married her."

Jess drew in a sharp breath, then asked, "Does everyone in town know about me?" Were they gossiping about her? And what she was doing here?

"That's what small towns are about."

"Oh, great." Jess closed her eyes. Had anyone seem her come out of the tack room after Hunter kissed her? Was she the fodder of gossip? She didn't want anyone thinking Hunter was bedding her. She didn't care about her reputation. It was in shambles anyway, but she did care about her job.

"Hey, Hunter," Ralph said.

Dang. Jess opened her eyes to see Hunter standing next to her and Ralph. Her face flamed because she hadn't even noticed the music had stopped and they were still dancing.

"Ralph. Evening, Jess." He inclined his head.

"Jess, this is my sister Margie." Ralph introduced

the two.

"So nice to meet you." Jess smiled at the young lady. Margie looked cute with her plaid shirt tied beneath her breasts, jeans and cowboy boots, her blonde hair pulled up into a pony tail.

"Hi." Margie's gaze never left Hunter's face. Oh, the poor girl had it bad.

The band struck up a new tune and everyone started to line up.

"Do you know how to line dance, Jess?" Ralph asked.

"No." Time to make a hasty exit.

"Time to learn." Hunter plucked her hand from Ralph's and pulled her away.

"Sorry Hunter, I didn't realize the lady was taken."

"I'm not."

"She is."

They spoke at the same time. Ralph grinned at them, and Jess glared at Hunter. "Later, Jess." Ralph grasped his sister's arm and walked away.

"That was rude, Hunter."

"So?"

"I never said I wanted to dance with you."

"You need to learn how to line dance."

"Don't tell me what to do." What was with him and this domineering attitude? "We're not on company time. You don't have the right to order me around."

"Wanna bet?" His eyes gleamed with devilishness.

Apprehension slithered up her spine. What was

he up to? He wouldn't make a scene, would he? She didn't think so. Before she could react he slid his arm around her waist and pulled her in line with him.

"Line dancing is really simple," he said as the music started. "Watch Susan, on the stage, to get the moves."

Jess glanced up to see her friend on the stage as she demonstrated the steps. It didn't look too hard, but it wasn't the dance she was worried about. It was being in Hunter's arms.

As the music started over, Hunter dropped his arm from her waist. Jess breathed a sigh of relief started to dance and ran right into Hunter's chest.

"Left, then right." He whispered in her ear.

Taking a deep breath, Jess gather her thoughts and concentrated on following the instructions being shouted from the stage. Step left, step left, step right, step right.

"That's it." Hunter whispered. "Relax and go with the music."

Jess didn't bother answering him. After a few minutes, she completed the dance without missing a step or running into Hunter again. The music stopped and pride swelled in her. She'd done it.

She let out a laugh and glanced up at Hunter with a smile on her face. "That was fun."

Her voice was breathy, her face flushed and her eyes danced with more accomplishment than Hunter had ever seen before. It was a heady combination.

"You haven't seen anything yet." He scooped her into his arms as the band began to play the Texas two step.

He whirled her around the room, continuing even when she missed a step or two. The crowd faded away as they danced. He focused on the joy he saw in her eyes, liking the way he could make her happy and danced.

"I've got to sit down." Her breathless voice reached his ears as the music died away once again.

How many dances did they have? He'd lost count. "This way, my lady." He curved his arm around her waist and led her to the table where Susan and Chris sat.

"You were great, Jess. I didn't know you knew how to two-step," Susan said as they sat down.

"I don't." Jess shook her head.

"She's a natural." Hunter scooted his chair closer to Jess. At least she was no longer avoiding him. Not that he'd given her much choice. But when they'd been dancing, something felt right. There was a chemistry between them and he wanted to explore it. His gut tightened. "Would you like a drink?"

"Yes, please. I'll have another beer."

"I'll get them," Chris said. He picked up the empty pitcher and walked away before Hunter could protest.

Hunter glanced back at Jess. "Beer? Somehow I pictured you as a white wine with a twist, kind of person."

"Oh God, no."

Susan laughed. "I've only seen Jess drink wine at the Dean's honor dinner."

"That's right." Jess grinned. "One sip and then I never touched it again."

"More beer," Chris announced, setting two pitchers on the table along with four full mugs.

"You're a doll, Chris." Jess grabbed a glass. "This is more fun than the frat parties we used to attend in college."

"Frat parties?" Hunter's gaze shifted from Jess to his sister, and back again. Jess had the mug in her hand and was downing the contents.

"Yeah." Susan gave a laugh. "We used to attend the best ones." Susan refilled Jess's glass when she set it on the table.

"Thanks, Susan." Jess grinned at his sister. "Watch and learn, cowboy." She picked up the mug and drained it once again.

Hunter stared at her.

"What's the matter? Never seen anyone chug-a-lug?" A grin played around her lips and her amber eyes were bright with mischief.

"Not a city girl." And that was the truth. His ex wouldn't touch beer.

"I told you I'm not your typical city girl. I've been around the block a few times. Heck more times than I want to count."

"Trying to prove how tough you are?"

"I'm trying to knock those prejudices out of your thick, hard head."

Chris laughed and Jess's smile grew wider. "See, Chris agrees with me."

"Jess used to drink the guys under the table in college," Susan told him filling Jess's mug with more beer.

"That was so much fun." A feline sneakiness

crept into her eyes.

Hunter's stomach clenched. His sister wasn't helping by refilling her glass. "I think you've had enough." He put his hand over the top of her mug, not letting her pick it up.

"I'm not on company time."

"Lighten up." His sister glared at him.

"She's on her third glass in the space of five minutes." He didn't care that his tone was angry. "Getting drunk will not prove anything." Why did he care? There were several clients from the ranch here, but it wasn't like they hadn't all let loose once in a while.

She pushed his hand away. "I'm not drunk. Not yet."

"Go for it, girl." His sister stuck her tongue out at him.

"Let's dance," Chris said as he stood, and took Susan's hand.

"Have fun, you two." Jess waved at them as they left the table.

"Guaranteed," Susan yelled back.

Hunter watched the pair before turning back to Jess. "Tell me more about these frat parties." Why did he care? Hell if he knew, but if he kept her talking then she couldn't drink. He placed his arm around the back of her chair.

"Nothing to tell." She sipped her beer this time, keeping her gaze on the dance floor.

"Oh I think there is." He couldn't stop her from drinking but at least she slowed down.

She set the mug down. "Judging me, cowboy? All

I ever did was dance and drink. Look, beer has a way of removing stress and frustrations." She glared at him and pushed his arm away. "And after these past few weeks I need it." She picked up the glass and drained it in the blink of an eye.

"A glass of water between drinks would be a good idea." He leaned back in his chair, so he had gotten to her this week. But he didn't like that she was trying to wash away the memories with alcohol. He'd seen too many idiot cowboys decided they could ride a bull after a few drinks and disaster ensued.

"Relax, Hunter." She poured herself another glass. Her hands steady.

He shook his head and pointed at her glass. "What are you trying to prove?" Dang this woman was tying him up in knots.

"Nothing. I'm hot and thirsty."

"Sizzling is more like it." Her face was flushed, the barn was warm, but not that hot.

She placed her hand on his shoulder, her breast pressed against his arm. "Dance with me, Hunter."

For once she wasn't pushing him away. It was the alcohol talking, but he didn't care. Capturing her hand, he held it then rose to his feet and tugged her out to the dance floor. At least out there she wouldn't be drinking. A slow ballad started, and he pulled her into his arms as they swayed to the music.

"You smell nice," she whispered, pressing close to him.

Her words caressed his skin, then she stood on her toes and her tongue tasted his ear lobe. His arms tightened around her waist. His blood pooled in his groin. "Do you have any idea of what you're doing?" God, he hoped so because he wasn't sure how much of her teasing he could take.

"Yes." Her tongue trailed down his neck, and then she rested her head on his shoulder.

Hunter stifled a groan as they moved to the music, her hips rubbed against his, her breasts pressed tight to his chest. Her arms entwined around his neck, fingers caressing the nap of his neck. The constriction in his jeans became unbearable.

This woman was more deadly than a rampaging bull. He fought against his rising desire. As much as he wanted her, now was not the time and place. Plus, he wanted her in full control of her senses.

"Jess." He tried to put some distance between them when she pressed against his erection. He was trying to resist his own desires, she had to give him some help.

"Yeah, handsome." She tilted her head back and gazed up at him with lust gleaming in her eyes. When she licked her lips, he had to bite back a groan.

Aw, hell. He couldn't do this. He shouldn't. She was drunk or close to being there and he didn't sleep with drunk women. But damn if that tongue of hers wasn't doing crazy things to his ear. Control flew out the barn door. He captured her mouth in a hard kiss, his tongue pushing its way past her lips to mate with hers. Her fingers tightened in his hair as she pressed her body against his. Their tongues danced to their own tune.

Hunter broke the kiss. Jess's head fell against his shoulder and ragged breathing filled his. Her eyes were closed as she rested against him like a limp dish rag. His erection pulsed against the confinement of his jeans. He needed to get them both out of there, fast, before they embarrassed themselves.

He searched the dance floor for his sister and Chris. He spotted his sister and nodded his head toward the door. Susan smiled and waved at him. Hunter glanced at Jess. Her eyes were open now and her face held a dreamy expression. Keeping her tight to his side, he half walked, half carried her out of the barn to his truck.

"Kiss me again," she demanded as he fumbled for his keys.

"You're drunk, Jess." He unlocked the passenger door.

"On you, cowboy." Her fingers curled around his neck and she tugged his head down. Their mouths met once again.

Hunter couldn't fight her. She tasted of beer and all woman. Before long they were both panting and the night air grew warmer. Laughter reached his ears. He needed to get them out of there. Jess wouldn't be pleased if she was the object of small town gossip.

His reputation could handle it, but not hers. Hurting Jess wasn't part of his plan. "Into the truck, Jess." He opened the door for her.

"Make love to me," she whispered.

A groan slipped past his lips. He wanted nothing more than to bury himself deep inside her warm willing body, but he wouldn't take advantage of her in this state. No matter what. He was a gentleman. But she was testing him by snuggling up to him and purring like a kitten.

"Make that offer again when you're sober and I won't refuse." He lifted her and placed her on the seat. "Time for all good little girls to be in bed." He fastened her seat belt before closing the door.

Hunter took a few deep breaths of night air, willing his erection to subside. The air cleared his head, but his erection throbbed with unfulfilled desire. Rounding the front of the truck, he got into the driver's seat and shoved the key into the ignition. His truck sputtered to life.

He wasn't a mile down the road when Jess released her seatbelt and slid across the bench seat to him. She laid her head on his shoulder while her fingers danced over his thigh.

"Jess, have a heart." His fingers clenched around the steering wheel. There was only so much a man could take.

"I'm not interested in your heart, even if you have one." She traced the bulge straining the fabric of his jeans. "Now this." She gave his erection a squeeze. "I'm very interested in what you're hiding here."

His hips jerked and the truck swerved. He swore beneath his breath. "Jess, I can't drive if you keep doing that." Thank goodness the roads were empty this time of night.

"Then pull over." Her tongue bathed his ear.

He swore out loud this time, braking the vehicle on the side of the road. After throwing the truck into park, he turned to Jess. He took her by the upper arms and set her away from him. "Get back on your side of the truck." His jaw clenched.

Her lower lips pushed out in a pout, but she did as he asked, even refastening her safety belt. Blowing out a breath, he put the truck back into drive. Several minutes later the truck skidded to a halt outside his house.

Snatching the keys from the ignition, he jumped out, jogged around the truck and opened the passenger door. His nerves were shot. His libido pulsed at him to take Jess to bed and fighting it took everything he had. Without a word he undid her seat belt and lifted her into his arms.

With one hand he opened his front door and kicked it shut, before striding down the hallway with Jess in his arms. She hadn't said word, just snuggled up to him.

"Where are we going?" she asked softly.

He gazed at her sleepy features. His breath caught in his throat. Damn, she was beautiful with her mussed hair, eyes dreamy, and lips wet.

"To bed." His voice was husky.

"It's about time." She smiled.

CHAPTER SEVEN

Jess groaned, rolled over, and squished her eyes shut from the bright sunshine. "Ugh," she mumbled as she pulled a pillow over her face. Her head pounded and her mouth was as dry as the hard packed Texas ground. This was why she'd given up drinking.

"Jess." Hunter's sleep-roughened voice stopped her movements.

Oh, hell, no. With dread filling her heart, she pushed the pillow off her face and opened her eyes to see Hunter leaning on one elbow, gazing down at her, his thick hair tousled, his chest bare, and...they were in bed together. *His* bed.

"Holy crap." She pulled the pillow back over her face. No, she couldn't have slept with him. Could she? She fought back the rising tide of nausea as she thought back to last night.

Beer. Dancing. Her and Hunter dancing. Kissing on the dance floor, then that kiss by his truck. A shiver swept up her body along with embarrassment. She'd taunted him in the truck, tracing his hardness as he drove. She remembered feeling giddy when he carried her from the truck to his bedroom. He placed her on the bed and then...nothing. Her mind was blank.

She groaned again as her stomach somersaulted. How long had it been since she'd gone on a beer binge? Probably since college. She obviously wasn't able to hold her alcohol like she used to.

"Are you alive under there?" A corner of the pillow lifted.

"No, I'm dead." If she was dead she wouldn't have to face him.

"Shall I join you?"

Was that humor in his voice? "Absolutely not." She threw the pillow in his direction and instantly regretted it as her stomach rebelled.

"Not quite yourself this morning?" The amusement in his voice danced over her nerves.

"Understatement of the year." She glared at him while willing her stomach to calm down. How dare he sit there looking like a cat who caught the bird. Her head hurt and her mouth tasted awful.

"Why don't you have a quick shower while I fix us some breakfast?" The mattress dipped as he rose.

The mere thought of food caused nausea to rise in her throat, but if it would get him out of the room, she'd agree to it. "A cup of coffee would be nice."

"Coffee and food. You need to eat." He sauntered around the bed and her heart pounded. Her eyes wandered over his shirtless torso and down to his jeans. Jeans? Oh, thank goodness. She forced herself not to back away when he leaned down.

"At breakfast you can tell me just where you learned to please a man like you did me last night." He dropped a quick kiss on her lips before strutting out of the room.

Oh crap, oh crap, oh crap. Jess sat up and pulled the sheet around her near naked body. Wait a second, near naked? She still had her panties on. Had they made love? Her head spun. Carefully she climbed out of bed and made her way into the bathroom.

She turned on the shower, took off her underwear, and climbed in. Her temples throbbed as she ducked her head under the shower head. Hunter didn't seem the type to re-dress her after they had sex.

How the heck was she going to face him? She didn't normally just fall into bed with a man. Despite her reputation for being wild she'd only slept with two men in her entire life, one guy at college and Ned. Well, now she could add Hunter to the list.

And she couldn't remember a darn thing. Pressing her palms against the tile, let the water flow over her. Sex with Ned hadn't been at all exciting and so easily forgettable, but Hunter's?

No, she had to remember. His kisses were wild and passionate. He was a man of deep passion. A sigh slipped past her lips. If only she could remember. She wanted to pound her head against the tile, not that it would help.

She vowed right then, no more alcohol. Turning off the water she stepped into the steam-filled room and grabbed a towel. Drinking had made her lose all control. After wrapping the towel around her, she turned to the sink. A new toothbrush, tooth paste, and a brush sat on the gleaming marble counter.

Did Hunter always have these things for his women guests? A giggle escaped her lips. At least one of them had some experience with the etiquette concerning one night stands. She brushed her teeth and pulled the brush through her wet hair. How could she escape breakfast with Hunter? Work? No, it was Saturday.

Maybe she could tell him she was meeting Susan to go shopping in Dallas. She shook her head. He'd just call his sister and say Jess was busy. She stared at herself in the mirror. Susan! She would know Jess spent the night with her brother.

"Well, Jess girl, you really messed up this time. You got drunk and slept with your boss. Kiss your job and dignity good-bye." Her stomach clenched in dread. She closed her eyes and moaned. She really couldn't blame Hunter if he did fire her. She'd certainly lost the bet they had.

She padded out to the bedroom, found her clothes folded on the chair, and pulled them on. She took her time tugging on her boots. Time to face the music and Hunter. She lifted her chin. She'd treat him like she always did, no different. Jess marched out of the bedroom.

Her steps faltered as she neared the kitchen. What was she going to say to him? Thanks for a wonderful night that I can't remember? A thousand butterflies and a few hundred elephants danced in her tummy. At this rate, she'd never be able to eat a thing.

She entered the kitchen and her heart jumped. Hunter was still shirtless, his muscles playing along his back as he cooked at the stove. The need to run her palms over those broad shoulders and smooth back almost overpowered her. Her breath caught in her throat. If she did, would he turn and pull her into his arms and kiss her into oblivion as he'd done last night?

Her knees went weak and she leaned against the door frame. Hot flames of desire licked at her body.

"Morning," he said as he turned from the stove.

"Morning," she mumbled trying to act as if nothing had happened. It was the only way she was going to make it through this breakfast.

"Come sit down." He gestured to the chair at the table. "I've got orange juice, coffee, and some French toast." He smiled at her.

"Have you ever been drunk?"

His hands stilled over the stove. "It's been a while."

She folded her arms over her breasts. "Then you should know how I feel about food about now."

"Nonsense. Best thing to get over the hangover." He pointed to the table again. "Take a seat and relax."

At least one of them was happy this morning. She shuffled over to the table, sat down, and focused on her hands resting on the table. Maybe, just maybe if she didn't look at him, she wouldn't feel the uncontrollable lust coursing through her veins.

Not looking at him didn't help. The sound of denim rubbing together as he moved teased her ears. The scent of pine and wood teased her nose. Oh, this wasn't fair. She waited for him to say more but he didn't. When was he going to tell her she was fired for improper conduct?

She jumped when his hand covered hers. Her head jerked up to find he'd taken a seat next to her.

"Nervous?" His thumb rubbed over the back of her hand. Goose flesh traveled up her arm.

She opened her mouth to give him a snarky reply

and her stomach growled. Heat filled her face.

"Someone's hungry." He picked up a fork with his free hand, speared a piece of French toast and brought it to her lips.

Jess's lips parted. Not that she had much of a choice unless she wanted syrup all over herself. The sweetness hit her tongue and she closed her eyes in bliss as she chewed. Her lids rose to see Hunter with another piece on the fork.

Her gaze was captured by his movements as his hand rose and he slipped the morsel between his lips. He let out a small groan as the fork slid from between perfect lips. She couldn't look away as he chewed and swallowed. The heat in his gaze singed her skin.

This was not good. So not good. "I..um...It's been a long time since I drank the way I did last night." The silence was killing her.

He didn't say a word. He only stared at her.

"Hunter, about last night." The words died in her throat.

"Last night was the best night of my life." He lifted her hand to his lips. "I've never been more satisfied."

Heat rose to her cheeks. This could not be happening. She tugged at her hand until he released it. Her fingers clenched in her lap. She couldn't look at him as tears sprang to her eyes. How could she have screwed this up? She loved working here. While it surprised her, she didn't want to mess up her job. She was just getting her life back on track and now it's back in ruins because of one stupid night. Heck, she even liked this macho cowboy. Yeah, liking him is what got her into this mess in the first place.

Swallowing the constriction in her throat, she lifted her chin. "I'll clean out my desk and the cottage and be out of your hair by tomorrow." Her voice was soft. What was she going to tell Susan? What did it matter anyway? Within a month she'd have nothing left if she couldn't pay the creditors Ned sicced on her. Where had that sobering thought been last night?

"There's no reason for that." He sat back, giving her some much needed breathing space. "Jess, what do you remember about last night?"

Hope filled her. He wasn't angry? "We danced and we kissed."

"We did. And after I placed you on my bed?"

Mortification shot through her veins. He couldn't let her leave with a little dignity in place? He had to drag it all out. "That's a little hazy."

His index finger trailed down her warm cheek. "Oh, Jess." He wiped away the tear on her cheek with his thumb. "Nothing happened last night."

"What?" Her jaw dropped open.

"We didn't make love last night." His voice was soft and soothing. "You were looking a little green. I was concerned, so I put you to bed and watched over you."

"But you let me think..." She pushed back her chair away from his touch. Dirty, rotten, stinking cowboy. Anger overtook her embarrassment. "How dare you let me think we slept together."

"But we did." He flashed her a charming smile.

"No, we didn't. You just said we didn't."

"I said we didn't make love. We did sleep in the

same bed together."

"A technicality." Relief hit her, along with a little bit of regret. Part of her was happy he was a gentleman and hadn't taken advantage of her inebriated state, the other wanted him to. What a mass of contradictions she was.

"In your book, not in mine." He pushed his chair back, stood, and paced around the kitchen.

"It doesn't matter." She stood. "You'll have my resignation on your desk by Monday."

"I didn't think you were a quitter, Jess."

"I'm not." She placed her hands on her hips. She really wanted to hate him, but her heart wasn't in it.

"What happened between us last night has nothing to do with your job. It was personal."

"It shouldn't have happened. Why did I allow myself a moment of weakness? I know better." She couldn't stay here any longer. To see him every day and feel the lust coursing through her body. No, it wouldn't work. "I can't say last night was the best night in my life because I can't even remember it."

A blaze started in his eyes and grew into a wild fire. Oh, why couldn't she keep her mouth shut?

He strode over to her and took her by the shoulders. "Last night was eye-opening." His gaze never wavered from her face. "And for your information, you're doing one hell of a job. You make things on the ranch run much more smoothly, efficiently, I haven't had one missed appointment or client since you came on board. I'm very happy with your work."

His words blew the anger out of her sails. He was

happy with what she was doing? "Thank you," she whispered. What was she going to do now?

"Look, Jess, I'm sorry I teased you about last night." His tone was soothing. "In my defense, you made it so easy to this morning. And you were hanging all over me last night, begging me to make love to you."

Her face flamed. "I'm sorry." Oh, criminy, now she was apologizing. When she forced down her wild side, life was simpler. It only got her into deep trouble when her wildness burst out. "Maybe I overreacted a bit."

"Friends?" He stepped back and held out his hand.

"Yes." She placed her hand in his. Her palm tingled from the warmth of his skin caressing hers. She breathed a sigh of relief. She still had a job. But couldn't she trust this new Hunter? Only time would tell.

His fingers tightened as he pulled her. Off balance, she fell into his embrace. "But soon we'll be lovers." He lowered his head.

Lovers. The word vibrated in her skull as her lips parted for his kiss. She should nip all thoughts of Hunter and sex in the bud, but her body had other ideas. It wasn't as if she cared right at this moment. She melted against him as flames of desire licked their way up her skin.

His mouth took control over hers, sapping her strength, making her surrender to him. Her arms rose and entwined around his neck. Her fingers found his soft hair.

His lips trailed from her mouth to her temple and she gasped for air. It wasn't fair. He made her feel like she'd been run over by a freight train. Very much like a stubborn, cowboy who wasn't going to take no for an answer.

She couldn't risk getting involved with him. Not with her debts, not with her fear of bulls. Those two thoughts were like a bucket of cold water. What was she doing?

"No." She put her palms against his chest. "We can't be lovers. Ever." She gave him a shove and he stumbled back. Jess turned and fled. She ran from him, from her own cravings, for her life. Emotions she thought long buried rose to the surface and her mind was in turmoil. Control. She had to find her control, over herself, over her body. Because she and Hunter could never be a couple.

****

The next day, Hunter tied Misty's and Zapper's reins around the post in front of Jess's house. He hoped he could convince her to go riding with him. After she'd fled yesterday, no one had seen her. Guilt ate at his gut.

He hadn't meant to hurt her when he teased about spending the night with him. Then there was that scorching kiss. She'd tasted of coffee and spice. A flavor he was quickly becoming addicted to. Hunter checked the food he'd put into the saddlebags before walking up the steps to knock on the door. A ride and a picnic was his peace offering. He could only hope she'd accept.

"What are you doing here?"

The door was flung open before he could make contact with the wood. Well, she wasn't happy, but he'd overcome greater obstacles. "I've come to take you on a date?"

"Date?" She crossed her arms over her breasts.

"Yes." He opened the screen door. The wariness in her eyes grew, but he wouldn't let it stop him, not just yet. "I want to put what happened yesterday behind us."

"I'm not sure I can do that." Her mouth pressed into a flat line.

"It's just a picnic lunch. Afraid of a few ants, city girl?" Fire snuffed out the wariness in her eyes.

"Ants don't bother me."

"Good." He grinned at her. "Go put on some jeans." He tilted his head to her shorts, but not before his gaze took in her toned bare legs. "Fried chicken is calling my name. And my source told me chocolate chip cookies are your favorite."

While her stance was closed, her eyes were still alight with fire. Time to up the game. "Afraid to be alone with me?" he challenged.

That did it. Her chin came up and her spine stiffened. "I'm not afraid of you. Give me five minutes." She shut the door.

Hunter smiled as he paced around the porch until she reappeared. "You couldn't manage to invite me in? After all I am sharing my fried chicken with you."

"I didn't think it was a prudent idea."

"You're probably right." He didn't like admitting it, but she was.

"Where's your truck?"

"We're going by horseback." He cupped her elbow. The color had drained from her face. He frowned. Something wasn't right. "Are you afraid of horses?"

"No." She shook her head. But unease clouded her eyes, making him question her quick response.

"Okay." He guided her down the stairs and over to the horses. She tried to tug away from his hold, but he just tightened his grip. Not enough to bruise her, but enough so she couldn't get away. "Misty's as docile as they come." He took her hand and placed it on the horse's mane.

Misty's ears perked up and she whinnied. Jess stumbled back and into Hunter's arms. Her face was even more pale and she was trembling. "It's okay," he whispered.

She took a deep breath. "I guess I'm not very comfortable close to horses."

"Then why did you come here to work? You must have known about the horses." He shook his head. It didn't make sense for someone not comfortable with livestock to work on a ranch. But then again, when did anything with Jess make sense.

"I needed a job." Her head tilted down, but her body remained stiff.

She couldn't tell a lie worth a damn. He cupped her chin and tilted her face to where he could see in her eyes. "The real reason."

"It is the real reason."

She stared him in the eyes. Maybe that was part of the reason but not the whole story. He'd dig into that later. Right now he wanted to get her on the horse.

"All right. Let's go riding."

"Are you joking? The horse is huge." She took a step away from him.

"Misty is only fourteen hands high and technically a pony. Think of her as a really big dog."

"Right." Her lips tilted up. "Just a big Alaskan husky."

"You got it." Hunter laughed and hugged her close. "Would you rather ride double?" He wanted to help her overcome her fear.

"You mean two of us on one horse?"

"Yep." He glanced down at her. She was no longer trembling and her face had some color to it.

"I don't know."

"This from the woman who said she wasn't afraid of anything." He'd make it a challenge, Jess couldn't resist a challenge.

"Is that a challenge, cowboy?"

"Are you accepting, city girl?"

She tugged from his embrace, took several steps over to Misty, her breathing short and choppy as she reached out a shaking hand to stroke Misty's neck.

"She's so soft." The amazement in her voice caused him to grin.

"Yes, she is. I make sure all the horses are brushed at least once a day. It helps keep their coats clean and smooth."

Misty lifted her head and shook it. Hunter caught Jess as she stumbled back again. "It's okay, she's just shaking her head. She likes what you're doing." Taking her hand, he put it back on the horse's neck.

With her hand beneath his, stroked up and down caressing Misty.

"How can you tell she likes it?" Jess asked.

He took her question as a good sign. "Look at her ears. They're bent and not pointing straight up."

"Yes. But...Oh. They just went straight up."

"She's listening. Happy horse bent ears, listening horse straight up, but if her ears are flat against their head, watch out, they're angry and unpredictable."

They continued to pet the horse for several more minutes. Jess's features took on a childlike glow, like a kid discovering something wonderful for the first time.

"Ready to ride?"

"No."

Her quick answer made him chuckle. "We are going to go on this picnic."

"Then let's take the truck, or better yet, walk."

"Ah, Jess." He rested his cheek against hers. "Where I want to go horses are the best choice. Trust me. I won't let anything happen to you."

"I don't know." Her voice was low and hesitant.

"The offer to ride double still stands."

"How would that work?"

"Let me take Misty back to the stable and grab a different saddle for Zapper."

"Zapper." She giggled. "What kind of name is that for a horse?"

"It's a perfectly good name." He nudged her over to Zapper. "Just pet him and I'll be right back." Hunter quickly untied Misty, and led her away. He reached the stable in record time, left Misty with one of the hands, and grabbed one of the bigger saddles.

He hurried back to Jess, who was in the exact spot where he'd left her, petting Zapper and talking to him quietly. He couldn't hear what she said, but Zapper was enthralled.

The Arabian-Thoroughbred wasn't as temperamental as some, but he did have his off days. Thank goodness today wasn't one of them. "Stay where you are," he said as he approached.

Since she was by Zapper's head, changing the saddle wouldn't be a problem and he didn't want her running away. In record time, he had the saddle changed, leaving the old one on Jess's porch.

"Okay, now I want you to put your foot in the stirrup," he told her as he positioned her beside the horse.

She placed her left foot where he told her to. "When I say go, swing your right leg up and over his back. I'll help you into the saddle."

"Okay." She took a deep breath.

Grasping her waist, he held her and said, "Ready, go."

Jess's knee buckled and they both fell to the ground. She began to laugh. Hunter glared at her for a second before chuckling. "That didn't go as planned." He stood and helped her to her feet. "Let's try this a different way."

"You mean we can take the truck?"

He ignored her hopeful tone. "Come on city girl, where's your spirit?"

"I left it in L.A."

Without a word, he marched over, picked up a

nearby heavy duty wooden box, and sat it next to Zapper. Then he mounted the horse in one smooth motion. "Let's take things slow. I want you to climb up onto the box with your back to me."

"I don't know about this," she said, but she did as he asked.

"I won't let anything happen to you."

"But..." She shrieked as Hunter lifted her off the ground. Zapper danced sideways as he set her down in front of him.

"It's okay." He soothed both horse and woman. "Jess, take your right leg and raise it over Zapper's neck."

"This is not a good idea." Her voice shook.

"It's fine." Her hands grasped his like a lifeline.

"We're so high off the ground." The anxiety was back in her voice.

"I'm not going to let you fall." And he wouldn't. He would protect her even from himself if necessary. He tightened his grip around her waist. Her unease surrounded them like a cloud. He wanted to help her over this fear.

She shook her head. Her spine as rigid as a fence post. He kept his tone even a low. "Do me a favor. Bend your right knee and raise it up."

She followed his instructions. He placed his palm on her inside thigh, ignoring the heat from her body, lifted her leg up and over the horse's neck.

Now to get her to loosen up. "See, that wasn't so bad was it?"

"This is crazy, Hunter." Laughter tinged her voice.

"Maybe, but I never said I was sane." Her butt pressing against his groin was causing parts of him to wake up and demand to play.

She giggled at his comment. Good. "Now, lean back against me and relax." Jess didn't budge. "Sweetheart, if you don't, this is going to be a very uncomfortable ride for you."

"You won't let me fall off?"

His breath was knocked out of him. "I promise, I won't let anything happen to you, on or off this horse. Trust me." His mouth was close to her ear.

Inch by inch, she melted against him. Hunter brushed a kiss against her temple, gathered the reins, and they were off.

CHAPTER EIGHT

After a half-hour, Hunter doubted his sanity. Jess's fresh scent filled every pore from her strawberry scented hair to the vanilla smell of her skin. She rested comfortably against him, her hands resting on his forearms as he guided Zapper.

"It's a beautiful day," Jess said.

"Yes." He was fighting his awareness of the way her lovely derriere rubbed against his groin. His erection pulsed with each step of the horse.

"How long have you owned the ranch?"

He was surprised at her question. "It was originally part of my father's ranch. He gave me five thousand acres as a present when I graduated from college." He transferred the reins into one hand. He could guide Zapper with his knees, but he'd rather keep the reins for now. He rested his other hand against her abdomen.

"Five thousand acres. That's a lot."

He smiled at the surprise in her voice. "Mom and Dad live about six miles north-east of the Double K. Their ranch is called Circle K and they still run it." He moved his fingers in small circles. Annoyance filled him because her clothing prevented him from feeling her silky skin.

"How big are the two ranches together?" Her voice hitched and he wondered if his touch caused it.

125

"About twenty thousand acres." He continued to stroke her stomach. Even through her clothing, her heat called to him.

"Isn't that a lot of land?" She wiggled against him.

"Not when you're dealing with cattle." Hunter nudged Zapper to the west. "Cattle need plenty of land to roam and graze."

Jess nodded. "I remember reading about that." She paused, then glanced over her shoulder at him. "Why does the brochure say one thousand acres?"

"That's just for the horses. I use two hundred acres for the bulls, and then the rest for cattle." He slid his hand to rest below her breasts. She puffed out a breath. "We're diversifying. Cattle, horses, bulls and we're going to be adding sheep." Her breath was coming in little pants. She was affected by him. Good. Satisfaction made him smile.

"I see." She shifted in the saddle and his erection noticed. "From my research, your prices for stud fees, training, and other things are pretty competitive."

"Yes." Why did her knowledge surprise him? She was a very smart woman, not like his ex who wouldn't even try to understand his business. "But you can't always predict how a horse will perform."

"Why wouldn't they perform?"

He let out a laugh. "Horses, even bulls, are like people. They have unique personalities and can be very stubborn."

"Great, does that mean Zapper might decide to take off with us on his back?" Her hands tightened around his forearms.

"Zapper is happy today, so no worries." He inched his fingers higher.

"What are you doing?" Her fingers encircled his wrist.

"What makes you think I'm doing anything?" He placed his palm back on her stomach.

"Because you've been stroking me for the past ten minutes."

He laughed, and then smiled. "Who, me?" He lifted his hand and ran a finger down her cheek before tracing her lips with the pad of his finger.

"If the shoe fits." Her fingers entangled with his.

He wanted to laugh, but didn't. Jess was so very different from his ex. Shana wouldn't ride with him, would never think about having a picnic lunch. No, Shana only saw him as a meal ticket. She wanted money and lots of it.

"We've talked about my family. What about yours? What does your father do?" He pushed thoughts of his ex-wife away.

"My dad is dead," she whispered.

"I'm sorry." He tightened his arms around her. The sadness in her voice was like a knife to his heart. "How long ago?"

"Since I was eighteen."

"And your mom?"

"My mom is around somewhere. Last time I heard from her she was living outside Sacramento in California."

"I'm sorry, I didn't mean to bring up painful memories."

"It's okay." She squeezed his fingers. "I miss my

dad, but nothing can bring him back."

"Any brothers or sisters?" It's funny Susan never mentioned any of this to him.

"I have a brother." Her voice grew lighter. "Ben is twenty-four and right now is in medical school." The pride in her voice came through loud and clear.

"I bet you two were a handful growing up." He could picture her running circles around everyone.

"We had our fair share of scrapes." She shifted. "I bet you were a terror growing up."

"I was a model child."

"Really? That's not what Susan says."

"My baby sister has been telling tales out of school again?" He tried to sound stern.

"She mentioned something about a frog in some girls lunch and a snake shoved down another girls shirt."

His laughter rang out. It was good to hear the lightness in Jess's voice. "I was ten. What else has my sister told you?"

"Oh, let's see. How she hid in the back seat of your car on the night of your big date."

"That's my baby sister, always butting in where she's not wanted." He smiled at the memory. "She popped her head over the seat just as I started to kiss my date. My little sister always had impeccable timing."

Jess's laughter was sweet music to his ears. But he wanted to know more about what made Jess tick. Heck, he wanted to know every square inch of her, inside and out. City girl or not, he like her spunk, her passion...he liked her period.

"What else do you and Susan talk about?" He guided Zapper into the meadow.

"Lots of things." She fell silent as he pulled the horse to a stop. Hunter allowed the reins to drop, then he dismounted.

"I'm going to help you off Zapper. So keep your feet in the stirrups and stand up." He held on to her waist. "Good, now lean toward me, and swing your right leg over the back of Zapper."

"Will this work?"

"I've got you." He braced himself as she swung her leg, took her weight, lifted her from the horse and set her on the ground.

"I did it." The surprise in her voice pleased him.

"That you did." He brushed a light kiss over her lips, but before she could react he stopped. "Go look around while I get stuff set up."

Jess took a few steps away from him and stopped. "This is beautiful." She waved her hand at the meadow, it's lush green grass, the trees that provided a natural shade, and the flowers.

"This is one of my favorite places on the ranch." He opened the large saddle bags, pulled out a blanket, the containers with their food, and some drinks. Taking the blanket, he spread it out between two oak trees, sat down the food, and went back to Zapper.

Hunter pulled the saddle off, set it on the end of the blanket, then led Zapper over into the shade where he could graze and rest. Jess was standing at the edge of the meadow looking out at the land below.

"Are you okay?" Her silence worried him for some reason.

"Fine. It's very beautiful. Peaceful."

"Yes." He came up behind her. "I love coming up here for the quiet, but also because I can look out at the land and feel proud."

"You should." She turned her head and glanced at him. "You run a very big operation."

"Yep. Come sit down." He took her hand and tugged her over to the blanket. Once they were sitting, he opened the containers, pulled out plates and utensils.

"I'm starving."

"I am too." But he wanted more than food, he wanted to taste those sweet lips again. Later, he promised himself. He filled her plate with chicken, salad and fruit before handing it to her.

She picked up the chicken leg and bit into it. His mouth watered, not for chicken, but for this woman.

"Aren't you going to eat?" she asked after swallowing her food.

"Yes." I'd rather eat you. *Slow it down, cowboy*, the voice of reason spoke in his head. He brought her out here to unwind and learn more about her, not to jump her bones. Not that he wouldn't mind a little hanky-panky, but it was her call.

She made him laugh and smile, something that had been missing over the past few years. She made him feel good. She held her own with him, not willing to back down when she believed she was right. Plus, she didn't let him get away with any macho crap. Jess must have been desperate to make that bet with him at the time. But now Jess was a woman who'd lost her way and was now finding it.

They ate in a compatible silence, with just the sounds of nature all around them. Hunter couldn't remember spending a meal without his date having to fill the silence with talking. He shook his head. Nothing Jess did was like any other woman he'd ever known.

She was the wild flower that blossomed in the desert or the filly who won every race even when she was considered out of the running. She was resilient, sexy, and damn smart.

"So tell me more about Jessica Sinclair."

"There isn't much to tell." A wall of ice formed in front of her, and he was determined to melt it.

"What did you want to be when you grew up?" Maybe some insight to her childhood would help him understand more about her as a complicated adult.

The silence grew and he was about to give up when she spoke. "When I was really little I wanted to be a teacher."

"You like kids?" He could see her getting down and dirty with a dozen kids. One day he'd have a family, he promised himself.

"Yes." Her eyes turned dreamy and soft. "I love kids. But when I found out I had to go through five years of intense college courses I gave up the idea."

"Somehow I don't see you flinching from a little hard work." Especially not after what he'd put her through and she succeeded with flying colors.

"When you're eight, five years is forever."

He chuckled. "So what about after you dismissed the teacher idea?"

"All the usual stuff." She set her plate aside.

"Nurse, actress, waitress, policeman, fireman, artist, mother."

"That's quite a list." A very eclectic list.

Jess ducked her head. "I was forever changing my mind. It wasn't until I was in high school I found something I loved."

"And what was that?" Her voice had changed and Hunter wanted to know what caused that wishful tone.

"Art," she said quietly.

"A woman who likes to work with her hands, I like that." His innuendo didn't go unnoticed. Her cheeks turned rosy.

"Hunter, I think..." Her words trailed off as she glanced up at him.

A connection sizzled between them. All the sounds faded away. Her heart shaped face filled his vision. His world had narrowed to this one woman, to Jess.

He reached out and ran his fingertips over her forearm. There was so much he didn't know about her, so much he wanted to learn. "Tell me more about your artist ambitions." Hunter took their empty plates and set them aside as he scooted closer to her.

"Why all the questions?"

She didn't pull back physically, but the ice wall was still there. "I want to get to know you."

"Why?"

"Isn't that what one does on a date?"

"Then I get to ask questions too."

"Ask away." Maybe if he answered her questions, she'd open up to him more.

"Did you always want to run the ranch?"

"Can't remember a time I didn't." Hunter laced his fingers behind his head and laid down next to her. "I loved working the land next to my dad."

"I bet it was great growing up here." She wiggled around until she was lying back, staring up at the sky through the tree canopy.

"It was. I loved every second of it. Have you always lived in the city?" He'd found an opening and he was going to take it.

"Most of the time. I grew up outside of the San Francisco Bay Area, then after college, Los Angeles."

""Do you miss the city?"

"Still testing me?" She rose up on her elbow and stared at him.

"Would I do that?"

"Yes." She punched him in the arm.

"Hey, that stung."

"You deserve it."

"I'll behave." He grinned at her.

"Yeah, right. When cows fly."

"You doubt me?" He sat up. She challenged him.

"You have a long way to go in learning how to behave, cowboy."

"Challenge accepted, city girl." Hunter grasped her around the waist, and pulled her on top of him as he laid back.

"See what I mean?" The laughter in her voice was music to his ears.

"Tell me about being an artist." Her laughter faded and the light in her eyes faded. He mentally kicked himself for destroying the mood.

"I like being able to create things."

"As in painting? Drawings? Creating art out of trash?"

He was pleased when amusement flashed in her eyes. "Painting and drawing." She braced her arms on either side of him. He barely held in a groan when her hips aligned with his.

"I've never had talent in that direction."

"I believe your talents lie with the ranch."

"True." He slipped his arms around her waist. "Why don't you get comfortable?"

"A little hard since you've got your arms around me."

"Really?" He applied some pressure, until she sank down against his chest. "Now you were saying."

"Impossible man," she mumbled, but laid her cheek against his chest. Her heat invaded his body making his sex throb. He parted his legs and cradled her closer. She tensed, then let out a sigh. "Susan said you hurt yourself in the rodeo." The words were soft.

"That's right." He looked up at the clear blue sky through the trees, not allowing the memories of that night agitate him.

"What happened?"

"You really don't want to know." He closed his eyes.

Her hair brushed his chin as she rose. His lashes lifted to see her concerned gaze on his face. If he raised his head, he could capture her lips and stop this line of questioning.

"Please."

Her please tugged at his heart. "Are you sure you want to hear this?"

"Yes."

"Okay." He curved his hand around her neck, and guided her head back down to his chest. If he was going to talk about that night, the least she could do was allow him to hold her, so he wouldn't feel so isolated.

"It was about three months ago. I was in Houston." His mind filled with the images from that night.

The smell of freshly turned dirt, horse flesh, manure, and the roar of the crowd. He hadn't slept much the night before. He was tired, damn tired, but he still climbed onto the back of the bull. He'd checked his rigging three times before he rode. With a nod of his head the chute opened.

"The bull was a rank one, but he was what I drew. Once the chute opened, Roundabout did his best to knock me off." The bull had twisted and turned doing his best to unseat his rider. "The buzzer sounded. I was elated. I made my eight second ride. I was about to hop off the bull when it happened."

Soft, tender fingers caressed his cheek. Jess was gazing up at him, her hand on his face. Her touch gave him the courage to go on.

"My hand caught in the rigging and before I could get loose the bull ran up against the arena fence. My leg was caught between the concrete and the bull." The gasp from the crowd and the yells of the rodeo clowns filled his ears. His leg twitched.

Jess trembled in his arms, bringing him back to the present. He bent his head and kissed her forehead. "It wasn't as bad as it sounds." He pushed away his melancholy.

"It sounds horrible and painful."

"Comes with the territory."

"Bull riding is a dangerous sport."

"It can be." He wanted to ease her tension. "I was lucky, there was an intern with the Justin Sports Medical team. He got to me and helped me. Without him it could have been worse." He remembered the young man, talking him through the pain as they took care of his leg. He'd been lucky, just some severely pulled tendons, and bruising. No breaks.

"And yet you plan to go back." She laid her head back down, but not before he saw the fear in her eyes.

"Yes. I have one more title to win."

"This year?"

"Yep. I've got the points and the money. As soon as doc gives the okay, I'll go back on the circuit and off to the NFR."

"NFR?"

"National Finals Rodeo. It's held in Las Vegas every year. Only the top fifteen cowboys in each event are allowed to compete." Thankfully he was still in the top fifteen, but he needed to get back out there.

"What's the appeal?" She ran her palm up and down his side.

"It's exciting." He drew in a deep breath as the thrill of conquering the beast raced through his blood. He loved being on the back of a bull, testing his skill against the animal. Or even training a bronco.

"I'm sorry, I just don't understand." She tilted her head concern clouding her eyes. "Why put yourself in a position where you could be hurt or killed?"

"It's man against beast. To see who can come out on top."

"In your case, the bull won." She pushed away from him, rolling onto her back.

Hunter rubbed his forehead. Jess was more uptight now than before. She was the one who wanted to know what happened, so why the change in attitude?

"Why can't a man be satisfied with what's in front of him?"

"What are you talking about?" He frowned. What had he missed in the conversation?

"You have your family, the ranch; you're doing something you love with the stock. Why aren't you happy? Why do you have to prove how much of a macho man you are?"

He ran his hand through his hair as he sat up. There was a catch in her voice. She was talking about more than him going back to the rodeo. "I'm not trying to prove anything."

"Men are always trying to prove something." She sat up and stared out at the meadow, but her eyes were unfocused, so he doubted she was even seeing it. "That's why men can't stay faithful to one woman. They always have to prove no woman is immune to their charm."

A two-by-four slammed up the side of his head. A man in her past had hurt her. He wanted to question her more about it, but her closed expression warned him off. She'd tell him when she was ready and not before. But right now, he wanted her to understand that, while bull riding was dangerous, he didn't take chances.

"I could just as easily be hurt here at the ranch." He kept his words soft. "Hell, I've hurt my hand worse chopping onions."

"That's an accident." She scrunched up her nose. "You deliberately put yourself on a bull. You dare him to buck you off. That's suicidal." She turned her head away, but not before he saw the tears in her eyes.

"Sweetheart." He cupped her chin and guided her face back around. Her tears sucker-punched him. He fought to breathe. "Don't cry." He slipped his arms around her, tugging her against him. The last thing he wanted was for her to worry about him.

"I can't help it." She sniffed resting her head on his shoulder.

"I know." He didn't know how to reassure her. He couldn't promise not to get hurt again, but he wouldn't take stupid chances. Not when he had her to come home to.

His head snapped up. This city girl had wormed her way into his heart. He wanted to spend time with her, to see her laugh and smile. To see her in his bed waiting for him. He hadn't expected this to happen, but it had. Hunter held her until her tears were spent, then pulled a handkerchief out of his pocket. With a gentle touch, he dried her tears.

"I'm sorry. I'm being very silly." She tried to pull away from his touch.

"You're being human."

"Maybe." This time she managed to tug away from him. "We should be getting back. It's getting late." She stood.

Hunter wanted to argue with her, but decided to bide his time. He was chipping away at the ice wall she'd erected. He'd learned a couple of things during their time together today. Some idiot broke her heart and she didn't want somebody in her life who lived a life in danger, like he did on the rodeo circuit.

Climbing to his feet, he began to gather up their meal. Jess helped him in silence, and within minutes everything was packed away. Jess was stiff in his hold as they rode back.

Two steps forward, five steps back.

****

Jess dropped the piece of charcoal back into its box as the early evening light streamed through the windows. She stared at the canvas. Hunter's smiling face stared back at her.

How had this cowboy wormed his way into her heart? She wandered over to the window and gazed out. While she couldn't see him, he was there with her. Today she'd lain against his hard body as they talked. The texture of his lips on her skin, the light caress of his fingers were sweet memories. And she wanted more.

A sigh escaped her lips as she leaned her cheek against the cool glass. Desire and need gripped her. Short of falling into bed with Hunter, she had to find a way to deal with these unreasonable emotions. Because she couldn't fall for a cowboy.

Just the idea of him climbing onto the back of a bull made her break out in a cold sweat. She shivered. Even if she told Hunter about her father, he'd still ride a bull. It was in his blood.

She'd heard it in his voice. The awe, the need to ride and win. Her fingers curled into her palms. No matter what she did to fight this attraction, this need, her efforts failed. He was going back to his bull riding and for as long as she lived, she couldn't watch another man she cared about be killed by a bull.

CHAPTER NINE

Snap out of it. A week later, Jess was frustrated with herself. Desire for Hunter still pumped through her veins. No matter how she tried to ignore it the attraction wouldn't fade away. And Hunter didn't help. Each day he made a point to come into her office for lunch, and then again as she was getting ready to leave for the day.

They'd end up talking and before she knew it they were having dinner together. The evening would end with hot, wet kisses that drove her to the point of losing control. Why didn't she just tell him to back off?

Maybe because his desire for her made the woman in her sing. And maybe because she wanted Hunter. He was wooing her. Now that they were past the outrageous flirting and power-play, she was finding him very hard to resist. But getting her heart broken by falling for a cowboy who could alter her life with one accident wasn't in her best interest.

Then there was her financial matters. She couldn't afford a complication such as a relationship with Hunter while she was still trying to straighten out her life. Time was getting short. Her little brother, Ben, would be starting his next semester of classes soon and he would need her financial help. At least for the moment she had the creditors off her back. As long as she paid them something they backed off. But her savings was almost gone.

A honking horn brought her out of her musings. She strode out of the office to see the vet, Mac, climbing from his truck. Curious, she made her way toward the barn. The vet had been out several times during the last few months.

Jess shivered in the coolness of the barn. Soon the Texas summer heat would be gone. According to Susan, the winters weren't too bad here. Making her way past the stalls, she saw Hunter standing outside Rainey's stall.

His lips were pressed into a flat line. He'd been trying to breed Rainey. Was he still having trouble? She padded up next to him and gazed into the stall. The vet was running a wand over Rainey's stomach. Then she noticed the machine next to the horse. An ultrasound machine.

"Easy, Rainey," the vet spoke softly as the horse shifted, then he patted her neck as he straightened. His expression was closed. Jess's stomach clenched, something was wrong.

"You were right on the mark, Hunter."

"Damn," he said.

"What's wrong?"

Hunter jerked his head toward her. "Sorry Jess, I didn't hear you come in." He glanced over at her. Tension hit her in wave after wave.

"What do you want me to do?" Mac asked.

"Let me check with Doug, but I think I already know the answer." Hunter ran his hand over his face.

"What's wrong with Rainey?" Jess watched the

two men remove the equipment from the stall.

"I'll call Doug," Mac said as he was leaving. "You need to explain to Jess." After Hunter closed the stall door, Jess placed her hand on his arm. "Hunter?" He was tense, like tempered steel.

"This isn't a good time, Jess." His gaze was bleak and her heart cracked.

"What is it? Is there something wrong with Rainey?" Hunter loved the horse. Heck, he loved all the stock. But he'd been trying to breed Rainey for a friend of his. The last time she was pregnant she'd lost the foal in the early days.

"Rainey's pregnant."

"That's great." When he didn't respond, she continued. "That's what you wanted, but clearly something is wrong. What is it?" It tore at her heart to see him so unhappy. He could confide in her.

Emotions warred on his face. Happiness, fear and regret. "Rainey is pregnant with twins."

"Twins? I didn't know horses had twins." She searched her mind but couldn't remember reading anything about it.

"They don't." He took her hand and led her out of the barn.

"What does that mean?" She was confused.

"It means one of the fetuses has to be aborted."

Her stomach cramped. "You can't let Rainey have both?"

He shook his head before taking her face between two cold palms, his chocolate eyes intense. "It's not safe for horses to have twins."

"But other animals do." She wanted to

understand, but her mind was still grappling with the word abort. Babies were precious little things. Oh, she respected a woman's right to choose. But this was an animal. It wasn't a choice Rainey could make.

"Yes, some animals do, but with horses it's not safe."

The way he held himself rigid spoke volumes to her. He didn't want to do this. "Can you tell me why?" Was asking him to talk about it pushing too hard?

"Let's go to my place. I need a drink." He released her and strode toward his home.

Jess followed. Hunter wasn't himself. The bright sunlight flooding his kitchen seemed out of place when the mood was so somber.

Hunter took a pitcher of ice tea out of the refrigerator, found two glasses and started to fill them. His hand shook.

Her strong cowboy was showing her another side to his complex personality. She slid up behind him, her hand covered his on the handle, and her other hand under the pitcher. Together the pitcher was lowered to the counter.

Her arms curved around him, her palms resting against his chest, as she pressed her cheek against his back. His body shuddered with each breath he took. "This is hard for you."

"Yes."

"You don't have to answer my questions." His vulnerability tugged at her heart. She wanted to comfort him. He needed her.

"I want you to understand. I don't do this lightly."

He turned within the circle of her arms. His hands spanning her waist.

"I'm listening." She held him close, sharing his pain.

"When Mother Nature created horses, she didn't make enough room in a mare's body to carry two babies. If I don't abort one of the fetuses, both babies will die and more than likely Rainey too."

She winced. "No way to help Rainey carry them to term?"

"No. It's not nature's way." He pushed her to arm's length, his gaze filled with regret. "If there was any way to avoid this, I would. Do you understand, Jess?"

"Of course I do." He'd never do something so drastic on a whim. She understood the gut wrenching choice being forced upon him. She raised her hand and caressed his face. She wanted to erase the heartache from his features, if only for a little while. "You're only doing this to save Rainey."

"Yes." He rested his forehead against hers, his warm breath caressing her skin. "I didn't think you'd understand."

"Why shouldn't I?" She let her fingers curve around his neck and tangle in his dark hair. Her heart hurt for him. A bond had grown between them, a bond she should be fighting against, but didn't have the will to combat.

"Some people who don't grow up on ranches or deal with horses don't understand. Some might consider it cruel and inhumane."

"You could never be cruel if you tried." Ned was

cruel. She'd seen him in action. Even after she broke off their engagement, it was close to impossible to break the hold he'd held on her life, but she was getting there. She wondered if Shana still had a hold on Hunter. Where did that thought come from? Hunter never talked to her about Shana. Jess only knew what Susan told her. Silence was a bad sign.

"I may not be a horse person, but you are." She caressed his head trying to soothe his anguish. "You're doing the best thing for Rainey. Would Susan or anyone else on this ranch think what you're doing is heartless?" Jess asked.

"No."

"Then why should I?" The anguish on his face began to fade with her words. She'd love to ask him about his relationship with Shana because she was getting the sense he hadn't been able to share the sorrows of ranching with his ex. But right now, Jess needed to be there for him. "I may not like the idea of having to abort one of Rainey's babies, but I understand the reality of losing all three. I would choose the same path you are."

His dark eyes brightened as he studied her and the thin line of his mouth relaxed. "You're one hell of a woman."

Jess smiled. "Tough decisions come with the territory. Trust me, I know." Her free hand covered her mouth. How could she have said that?

"What do you mean?" He tightened his hold on her waist when she squirmed.

"It's nothing." She lowered her gaze, shutting out the questions his eyes begged her to answer. She mentally kicked herself for revealing something so personal.

His fingers curled around her chin, lifting it until her gaze met his. "Talk to me, please."

His soft spoken words cracked the ice around her heart. "I made a tough decision before coming here." She swallowed trying to ease the constriction in her throat.

"How?" He trailed his hand from her chin to the nape of her neck caressing her tense muscles.

"I was engaged." The crack became a fissure. "I walked out on my fiancé." Walked? Hell, she'd run. Not because she was scared of Ned, but because she knew it was the right thing to do. So she'd run as far and as fast as she could.

"You still love him." His face tightened.

"I wouldn't love that lying, cheating, two-timing piece of cow dung if you paid me." She took a deep breath. A weight lifted from her shoulders. She'd exposed her ghost to the daylight only to find it wasn't substantial.

"That bad?" A twinkle flashed in his eyes and his features softened.

"I found Ned in bed with his female business partner." She bowed her head. Even though it no longer bothered her that Ned chose his blonde haired partner over her, she didn't want to see the pity in Hunter's eyes.

A soft swear word, followed by the tightening of his arms pulling her in for a tight embrace, comforted her. "He's an idiot."

She risked taking a peek at Hunter's face. There

was no pity, only rage. Catching Ned in an affair was only part of the scenario. "You think I'm a fool?"

"Hell, no. He's the damn fool." He took her face between his hands, keeping her gaze locked with his. "You're a beautiful, intelligent woman, Jess. Any man who diminishes your radiance deserves to be shot."

Tears filled her eyes. The monkey was partially off her back. Later she'd tell him the rest of the story including her debts. And she'd have to tell him about her father's death. Her heart squeezed in her chest and she turned her head away. She was so wrong for him. She had too much baggage for Hunter.

Warm fingers cupped her chin and turning her face back to him. "No tears." His calloused thumb brushed the wayward tear away.

For the first time in a long time, someone saw her as a woman, worthy of praise and attention, even after she'd done so much to push him away. "You're so good to me," she whispered.

"Nice to know I'm good for something." He hugged her close, his lips at her temple.

His embrace lightened her spirit. Her failed relationship floated away and now she was looking toward the future rather than back at the past. But what had he meant, that he was good for something? Clearly his failed marriage had done a number on his self-esteem. That was unexpected. Hunter was such a confident man.

Hunter leaned against the counter, pulling her between his legs, and she melted against him. She enjoyed his arms around her. Her heart pounded in her chest as liquid fire ran though her veins.

"I think you're good for a lot of things," she whispered.

"And so are you." He brushed a kiss over her temple. "You're a great office manager, a good kisser, and I know you'll be a fantastic..." He lifted his head and their gazes clashed. "Lover." The word barely left his lips before he captured her lips in a deep kiss.

She didn't even hesitate to part her mouth for his. Their tongues tangled. He tasted of wickedness, a wickedness she wanted to explore, and also full of promise. There was danger there as well to her heart, but she ignored the warning bells clanging in her head.

His fingers wove into her hair as they kissed. He pulled the pins allowing her hair to cascade down around his fingers.

"I love your hair." He broke the kiss to whisper against her lips. "So soft, so silky. I lie awake at night thinking about how your hair will feel against my naked skin." His gaze met hers and the fire burning in the dark depths of his eyes sent a shiver of excitement through her veins. "And your lips all over my body."

A tide of desire hit her with the force of a tsunami. She leaned into him. He nibbled his way to her ear and tugged the lobe before bathing it with his tongue.

"You taste like a fine wine. Aged to perfection," he whispered.

Heat pooled between her legs. His erection pressed against her and she shifted her thigh against his. How would it feel to give in to this desire? This need?

"We shouldn't do this," she whispered, her willpower disappearing in a puff of smoke.

"I don't have the strength to stop." His words were choppy. "I need you."

"I need you, too." She savored the feminine power she held over him, but they were in this together.

His nails scraped over her breasts. She arched into the sensations, but he didn't stop there. He continued sliding his hand down her body until he cupped her through her jeans.

"Hunter." She cried out his name as her knees went weak. Her fingers tightened around his shoulders to keep from melting into a puddle at his feet. The overwhelming need to strip off his clothes and do wild wicked things to him took over her entire being.

"I love that I can take your breath away with just a touch." His fingers traced the seam of her jeans.

Her hips jerked in response. She wanted to beg him to continue...not to stop. Her body screamed at her to let him continue, while her brain yelled stop. Her body shook with the tingling sensations coursing through her nerves. Oh, the hell with it. She was going to follow her body's lead.

She slid her hands down the muscles on his back until she encountered denim. Her fingers tunneled beneath his jeans. Finding the tail of his shirt, she pulled. She needed to touch his bare skin.

His abdomen contracted as she lifted his shirt and trailed her fingers over his skin. Flames licked at her palms. Her skin burned like hot coals. But she didn't care. She couldn't resist the temptation to see him. All of him. Their bodies parted. Jess whipped his shirt over his head and let it fall to the floor.

She sucked in a breath at the sight of his magnificent chest. A smattering of fine dark hair tickled her palms, but didn't take away from his beauty. Reality was a heck of a lot better than her wild imagination.

"Your turn."

Before she could comprehend his words, her shirt was whisked off and her bra followed seconds later.

"Glorious," he pulled her back into his embrace.

Her nipples hardened when they came in contact with his hair-roughened chest. She wanted to rub herself all over him. She glanced at him to find his smoldering gaze on her.

"You are the most beautiful woman God ever created."

Her skin flushed. His words made her feel so cherished, so alive, so loved. "You're not half bad yourself, cowboy."

He flashed her a wicked smile before taking her lips once again. This time his kiss was harder, more passionate. He tasted of sin and sex. An addicting combination she wanted to drink until she was sated.

She loved the feeling of his muscles playing against her hands as they moved over his chest. His stomach jumped as her fingers skimmed over the top of his jeans. She found the snap, undid it and lowered the zipper.

His erection pressed against her hand and a shudder ripped through her body. Lord, she wanted this man. Hunter widened his stance, giving her greater access. The fingers of her right hand slipped beneath his boxers.

Hot steel nudged her palm. He was so hard. So needy. She used her nail and ran circles over the head of his bulging erection.

"Minx," he growled the word against her lips, before lifting his head. "Two can play that game."

She shivered when the button on her jeans gave way, then the zipper. Her muscles contracted as he pushed his palms beneath the denim at her hips. Fabric pooled around her boots.

"Oh God," he said. "A thong, you had to be wearing a thong."

She giggled, but it turned to a gasp as his finger slipped beneath the fabric and slid into her feminine core.

"So hot, so wet." His lips caressed her collar bone before moving to her breasts. His teeth grazed over one nipple then moving to the other.

Her fingers tightened on his sex. "Make love to me, Hunter."

He stilled as the world fell silent. She cursed herself for voicing her need. She closed her eyes and rested her forehead against his arm.

"Look at me, Jess." His voice was strong and firm.

His voice commanded obedience. She tilted her chin and they were practically nose to nose. "Are you sure you want this?"

She nodded, not trusting her voice.

"If we make love, there will be no going back."

"I want you."

Without a word, he removed his hand from her sex and lifted her into his arms. The walk from the kitchen to his bedroom was fast. She barely was able to take a breath when she was sat down on the mattress.

He knelt at her feet. First he removed her boots, then socks and finally her jeans. His calloused hands caressed her calves before moving up past her knees to her thighs. She squirmed on the bed. "Lay back." She didn't even think about not obeying him. Instead, she fell onto her back, surrendering to the moment. His fingers curved around the fabric of the thong and it was whisked off her body.

Molten heat flowed over her as her fingers clenched the bedspread beneath her. She pulled at it to shield herself from his gaze.

"No." He stilled her movements. "I want to look at you."

Trapping her lower lip between her teeth, she gave a nod.

"So beautiful."

Jess opened her eyes to see Hunter gazing down at her body. He didn't seem turned off by her small breasts or large thighs. She watched his face for any sign of displeasure, Ned had always pointed out every imperfection.

"God broke the mold when he made you," he whispered. His smile was as sinful as Godiva chocolate, and she couldn't help but smile in return.

She started to sit up. "Your turn."

"Not so fast." He put his hand on her shoulder. "I want to enjoy the womanly attributes before me."

Her whole body throbbed as he sat down on the cream-colored chair, removed his boots and socks, then stood and slipped off his jeans. His erection tented his boxers briefs. Her stomach tightened. Need gnawed her insides, eating away at her sanity and control.

The mattress dipped when he knelt on it. His heated gaze sent tiny fissions of pleasure through her. His palm covered one breast, and a breathy moan escaped from her lips.

"So soft, so beautiful, I must taste." His voice was husky. He lowered his head and his mouth replaced his hand. Jess arched her back into his mouth. Oh. Dear. God. His tongue danced over her nipple, toying with it, creating delicious shivers to shoot straight to her core.

Her fingers curled into his hair, holding him to her while he tormented her. His head rose, and she caught a glimpse of a wicked grin before his head dipped again. He kissed his way down the center of her breasts, to her stomach causing her to lose her hold on his head. His tongue laved her belly button before moving on.

When he reached the top of her mound she whispered, "You can't."

"Easy, sweetheart." His hot breath caressed her skin as he spread her legs.

He drew a finger through her dewy softness and she cried out. His touch set her on fire, and she wanted more. He licked her outer lips and she let out another cry of pleasure.

His palms pressed against the inside of her thighs,

keeping her legs parted as he continued to love her with his tongue. She wanted to beg him to stop, and to continue, all in the same breath.

She clenched her fingers around the bedspread as liquid volcanic heat flowed from her core through her veins. Her stomach tightened like a spring. The tension held steady until she was perched on the edge of the unknown.

Her toes curled as an explosion hit her with the force of a charging bull. Her entire being lit with pleasure. Her core throbbed, her skin tingled, and she wanted more.

"You are so very responsive," Hunter said as he gazed up at her.

"I've never..." Her head went from side to side. She'd never achieved an orgasm easily, but with Hunter it was there before she knew it.

"May that be the first of many." He rose over her as his lips captured hers.

Her own spicy flavor burst upon her lips. She wanted to taste him, to make him explode as she had.

"I..." She drew in deep gulps of breath.

"Shhh." He ran his finger over her lower lip. "This is for you. Only you."

His manhood pressed her stomach. When had he taken off his shorts? He loomed over her, and she glanced down. Her mouth dropped open. He was hard and big. She swallowed.

"You're magnificent," she whispered.

"Just for you." Her gaze followed his hand as he reached over to the night stand and pulled the drawer open. Then there was a condom between his fingers.

"Allow me." She plucked the packet from his fingers, ripped it open and then slid it down his hard shaft. "So darn big."

"I'll take it slow and easy." He aligned his shaft, and pressed forward.

Her neck arched as he pushed into her wanting core. Lust, need, and love boiled to the surface. Hunter's gaze never left her face, desire turning his brown eyes to bronze.

"More," she whispered, her arms rising and encircling his back.

"Your wish is my command." His lips captured hers as he thrust forward.

She cried out into his mouth in pleasure. Sweet, sweet, pleasure. Her nails curled into his skin as he began the sweet torment of penetration.

With each thrust the pressure built inside her. Their lips tasted and nipped at each other's skin. Her hips rose to meet his. Her world was flying out of control. A moan escaped and her body broke free as passion ran wild through her veins.

"Your turn," she whispered, trying to catch her breath.

"One more, sweetheart."

"I can't take anymore."

"Oh yes, you can." His hot breath fanned her skin. Their rapid breathing filled the room as he continued to love her, taking her higher and higher.

He wormed his hand between their bodies, his thumb finding her nub and caressing it. "Hunter," she screamed and she tightened around him.

"That's it." He thrust several more times.

Her nails dug into his back as she shattered into a million pieces, and within seconds he followed. His own release made her core pulse even more.

"You're mine," he whispered, before collapsing over her.

His skin was hot against hers, and she didn't regret a second of this. She was falling for this cowboy. Caution be damned.

CHAPTER TEN

Hunter gazed down at Jess while she slept. A sense of satisfaction permeated his body and mind. For the first time in his life he was sated. Jess held nothing back from him. She'd tested his limits and pushed him beyond.

Sex with his ex had been good, but the second he got off, Shana had gotten out of bed and into the shower, washing off his touch. Not Jess. She'd protested when he stood up to get rid of the condom. Then when he came back to bed, she'd cuddled into his arms. So affectionate. He loved that about her. She'd fought him tooth and nail, but now she was his.

He tightened his hold on her. Somewhere along the line their relationship had crossed the boundaries from playful flirtation to commitment. He didn't sleep with just any woman who caught his fancy, despite his reputation as a flirt. He especially didn't sleep with female employees, even if the ranch didn't have many. He had his principles, but had to admit they'd somewhat flown out the window today.

Jess had gotten to him from the start. Her sexy mouth challenged his authority and she defied every notion he had about city women. She'd proven herself ten times over. There was still about month left in her trial, but the test no longer mattered. He was going to keep her around.

Sudden dread filled his gut. His heart thumped in his chest. Until today, he hadn't really thought what it would mean to have Jess stay on the ranch. She was a part of him now and he wasn't going to give her up. There were so many facets left to explore. But first, he needed to find out more about her past.

What if she wouldn't stay? She hadn't told him everything. He sensed something lurked in her past and that mystery was a disaster in the making. While she'd talked about her ex, he suspected there was more to it. Besides, he wanted to know everything about her before he asked her to be his wife.

Wife? Hunter drew in a shaky breath. He'd never thought about getting married again, at least not before he won his championship buckle. And even if Jess was willing to simply live with him, his sister and the community wouldn't let him get away with it.

There was something about Jess he'd noticed as they'd made love. She wasn't as experienced as he'd thought she might be. The wonder on her face when she'd come apart in his arms. He'd never felt such a connection to a woman. What they shared was rare and he wasn't about to give it up. If he had the chance.

Her eyes fluttered. "What time is it?"

Jess's groggy voice had him smiling. "Almost eight. Go back to sleep." He stroked her silky hair until her breathing evened. Tomorrow would be soon enough to make plans.

****

"I must say I haven't seen you this happy in a long time," Susan said to him a week later.

"That's because I am." Hunter watched the horse

being worked in the arena. "Doc gave me a clean bill of health, so now I can get back to training." He glanced around looking for Jess. They'd been together every night and she'd promised to come down and watch him train.

"Does it have anything to do with our office manager?"

"Yep." He smiled, thinking back to last night. Hunter had stayed with a sick mare until late in the evening, when he arrived home, tired, smelly and ready for bed, Jess had been there. She sat on his sofa wearing nothing but a pair of boots and one of his cowboy hats. His weariness faded the second he laid eyes on her.

"I knew Jess was the right woman for you," his sister commented.

He wanted to argue with her, but she was right. Jess was perfect for him. The only problem was that anytime he brought up her past or he tried to talk about anything more permanent, she refused.

Last Saturday night, he'd made plans to drive into Dallas and take her to a nice restaurant, followed by dancing, but when he told her about it, she refused, insisting she didn't need to go out, she was perfectly happy on the ranch. He was glad she appreciated the ranch but what was up with refusing to visit Dallas with him for a special date? He couldn't figure her out, and it was making him worry about what lurked in her past. Damn it he wanted all of her, not certain pieces.

Monday he'd had flowers delivered to her. Jess had smiled, told him they were beautiful, but unnecessary. No matter how he tried to show her she meant something to him, she'd brush his gestures off.

Unless they were in the bedroom, of course. There she'd cuddle up to him, rub her cheek against his chest like a kitten looking for attention. Her lips would trail from his chest to his groin then, like any male, he was a goner.

"Don't drool over my best friend in my presence." Susan smacked him in the arm. "But seriously, I'm happy for you."

"Thanks, Sis." He hugged her.

"I'm glad Jess finally told you about her past and you understand."

"What about it?" He wasn't proud but he was going to pump his sister for information. "She told me about her ex." Not that she said much.

"Good." Susan's expression was guarded.

"She told me she found her ex in bed with his business partner."

"Yeah, that was the least of what he did to her."

"What else did he do?" Hunter froze. Had Ned hit her?

Susan shook her head. "Ask Jess, it's not my story to tell."

"Susan." He tried using his best 'you will obey me' voice.

"No, sorry, brother."

Hunter sighed. He wouldn't get anything out of his sister. The dread returned. What was Jess hiding? He'd tried countless times to get her to talk about what was bothering her, but she shook her head and said it was nothing. How bad could it be? His imagination filled in some ugly scenarios, and the worst one of all was the one where she walked away from him.

"Where is Jess?" he asked, talking around the knot in his throat. He struggled to pushed away the bad vibes. He didn't need this before is practice bull ride today. His mind needed to be on task.

"In the office. She was on the phone with one of the rodeos about our stock contract. Want me to go get her?"

"No, I will." He was almost to Jess's office when he heard her raised voice. It wasn't like Jess to raise her voice to anyone. On high alert, he stepped into the doorway.

Her back was too him, but she was stiff and her fingers curled around the phone cord as if she wanted to strangle it. It hit him then. He'd never seen Jess with a cell phone.

"Look, I told you I'd pay half."

Half? Half of what?

"No, I will not take responsibility for someone in your company not verifying the facts."

Her back stiffened as she listened to the person on the other end of the phone.

"Yeah, fine. You go ahead and try that." She slammed the receiver. "God, what did I do to deserve this mess?"

"Want to tell me about it?"

Jess jumped, whirled around, and her gaze met his. "Hunter, I didn't hear you come in." She smiled at him, but it was a taut smile.

"Who were you talking to?"

"It doesn't matter."

"I think it does." He marched over to her. She was keeping secrets and secrets, in his experience, led to nothing but trouble.

"It's a personal matter." She touched his shoulder. "I'm sorry, did I miss your ride?"

"No." He tilted his head and placed his hands on her waist. "Tell me about the call? What I can do to help you?"

Jess shook her head. "You can't help. It's personal." Her chin came up as she glared at him.

"Anything that affects you, affects me."

"Not this."

"Let me help you." Hell, he was practically begging her, but he needed her to understand he wanted to help her. If only she would share her burden.

"I'm sorry Hunter, but this is really none of your business."

"Dang it, Jess." He pushed away from her. "Why won't you discuss this with me?" Did she not trust him? She trusted him with her body, but not much else, and he didn't like it at all.

"Because I need to deal with it on my own without help."

"I understand, but I thought we were partners." She shifted from one foot to the other before her fingers curled into her palms. He needed to back off before her anxiety went off the charts. "You can talk to me anytime. You know that, right?"

She blew out a big breath and nodded her head. As much as he wanted to hash this out, he'd let it drop for now. "Okay, let's get to the arena. Everyone is waiting." He took her cold hand in his and led her from the office, his gut in knots. She didn't belong to him, not fully. Would she ever? The question played tag in his mind.

Once at the arena, he dropped a hard, quick kiss on her lips before he turned and walked to the chute. He closed his eyes and concentrated on the job to be done.

****

Jess's gaze followed Hunter's retreating figure. She'd deflected his questions once again, but it wouldn't last for long. She'd almost broken down in the office and confessed about her debts, but at the last second she held back. She wouldn't involve him in her money problems. Those were hers to solve. She was the fool who'd let it happen. She owned it.

"Don't worry, Jess. Hunter's done this hundreds of time," Susan said from beside her at the fence.

"Why would I worry?" Hunter told her he was going to ride now that he'd been given the okay from his doctor. She thought it was a great idea. Most of the hands were gathered around the arena. What was she missing?

"He didn't tell you, did he?"

"Tell me what?" Jess frowned. She'd noticed a gated fence, but...her heart stopped.

"He's going to ride a bull."

Jess's gazed locked on the steel gate. Any words she had in her mouth dried as the door opened and the bull jumped out, with Hunter on his back. Her heart lodged in her throat as the bull kicked up all four of his hooves in the air before finding the solid ground, only to launch again.

How could she watch this? But she couldn't tear her gaze away from Hunter's on the back of the beast, his body undulating in perfect timing with the bull. She muttered a prayer for Hunter's safety.

She studied him for any signs of distress. His eyes were practically closed, his lips compressed into one thin line. One hand tightly gripped the rope around the bull, the other waved in the air. His thigh muscles bulged as they gripped the bull's sides.

Eight seconds. That's all he had to stay up there for a successful ride. She flinched when a whistle went off. Two hands ran into the area and Hunter smiled for the first time. Jess drew air into her lungs. The ride was over, Hunter was going to be okay.

The bull gave one last spin and Hunter went flying through the air. Silence followed the sickening thud of his body hitting the ground. Then there was action everywhere. Chris and Cal ran to Hunter, the other hands coaxing the bull out of the arena.

"Jess." Susan's voice was quiet.

"I can't see him." Jess started to climb the railing of the area, but Susan's hand on her shoulder kept her in place.

"He'll be okay."

Her stomach cramped. "But I can't see him." She tried to keep the fear from her voice, but failed.

"The boys will take care of him."

Damn, why did these cowboys have to be so tall? "What are they doing?" Her voice rose. How bad was he hurt? Where was the ambulance? This couldn't happen to her a second time in her life, could it? She couldn't lose another person she loved to a bull.

Loved? Oh, God. Her knees went weak and she clasped the wood railing. Why hadn't she seen it before? She'd been sleeping in Hunter's bed for a week now, and somehow he'd woven his way into her heart.

But she wasn't the right woman for him. He needed someone born and raised on a ranch. Someone who wasn't in so much debt it would take her years to pay it off, not to mention having a brother to support through medical school. Hunter needed someone who could watch him ride and win his championship.

This horrible moment made one thing very clear. She wasn't cut out for ranch life, and it was time she accepted it. Tomorrow, she'd start looking for a job in Dallas. She hated the idea of going there because the city was where Ned could find her. But she was a good office manager, and the city offered jobs.

"It will be okay, Jess," Susan said in a soothing voice.

"Yeah, that's what they said when they carried my dad out on the stretcher." Where was the emergency personnel? "He died before I could say good-bye." She had to see Hunter, now.

She pushed Susan's arm away, climbed the fence and sprinted for the line of cowboys. She pushed at them, but they wouldn't budge.

"Let her through," Chris said.

The long-sleeved, dark-shirted wall parted. Her knees wobbled, but she forced herself to stay upright. Hunter lay on the ground, his eyes open, his lips parted, as he took in big gulps of air.

Jess dropped to her knees next to him. Tears filled her eyes, and she couldn't even speak. Fear filled every fiber of her being.

"I'm okay," Hunter said, his voice scratchy. "Got the wind knocked out of me."

She blinked at the spots dancing before her eyes.

"Jess?" His calloused fingers against the back of her hand jolted her back to reality.

"Hunter." She turned her hand over and their fingers entwined as her tears dripped onto them.

"It's okay, sweetheart." His free hand touched her shoulder, urging her down against his chest.

She laid her head over his heart. Her fear receded with each strong beat. He was alive. Sobs racked her frame.

"She's in shock."

Hunter's voice barely registered. She wanted to deny his words, but her throat was blocked.

"I'm okay, sweetie," he crooned.

She hated how her fear made her lose control. Hated that Hunter would risk his life riding a bull. Hated the fact that he was right. She couldn't fit into his life.

"Baby." His fingers ran over the back of neck trying to soothe her.

"No." She rocked back on her knees, dislodging his hand. "I can't do this. I just can't." Jess surged to her feet and ran, as fast as she could.

****

Hunter struggled to his feet.

"Easy, Hunter." Chris grabbed him by the arm as

167

he swayed.

"I need to get to Jess." The look in her eyes, the pure unfiltered fear sent a chill straight to his heart.

"You need to see doc."

"I'm fine." He took a step and his knee buckled.

"Yeah, right." Chris and Cal caught him.

Hunter cursed. He hoped he hadn't reinjured his knee. "Susan." He looked around for his sister.

"I'm here." She stepped up beside Chris.

"Go after Jess. Talk to her. Let her know I'm all right." And he would be. He refused to believe anything else.

"I'll try. She's really scared."

As his sister jogged away, Hunter looked up at the sky praying for divine intervention. Then he said to Chris, "Get me to doc's." The sooner he saw doc, the sooner he could get back and show Jess everything was great.

****

"Jess?"

"In the bedroom," Jess yelled. She pulled another shirt off the hanger and threw it into the suitcase lying open on the colorful bedspread.

"Running away isn't going to help anyone." Susan lounged against the door frame.

"True, but since I don't belong here, it doesn't really matter, does it?" Jess squared her shoulders.

"How can you say that? You needed someplace to recharge after what happened. And you love it here."

"Sure, like cows love to be branded." Jess paced from the closet to the bed and back again. Yes, she loved the Double K. Who'd have thought she'd fall in love on a ranch in Texas?

"Sarcasm is a poor substitute for the truth. Come on Jess, what is really going on?"

"Nothing." She couldn't meet Susan's gaze. If she did, she'd spill the beans.

"Bull. We are best friends, right?"

"Yes," Jess mumbled. Susan was worse than a Cairn Terrier chasing a cat when she got an idea in her head.

"Then talk to me. Why are you freaking out?"

Jess faced her friend and crossed her arms over her churning stomach. "Remember I told you in our first year of college that my dad died."

"Yes."

Jess sucked in a breath. "My father was a bull rider. He was killed by a bull."

Susan's eyes grew wide and her mouth opened, but no words emerged. "Oh, my God," Susan whispered. "Why didn't you tell me?"

"At the time, it was too painful. Later, it didn't seem to matter so much." Jess paced. "Dad loved bull riding and the rodeo."

"Have you told Hunter?"

"Only that my dad is dead, not how." What good would it do? Nothing would or could change the facts.

"Why not?"

"Because Hunter is a bull rider. It's a part of him. A part I can't share." It was time for her to leave. She couldn't be the woman Hunter wanted or needed. She could never stand to watch him on the back of a bull again.

"Hunter won't care about that."

"Even if he doesn't, I can't sit at home waiting while he's out riding bulls." Jess shook her head. "Besides, there's still the issue of my debt."

"My brother isn't so shallow to care about a few credit cards."

Jess sighed. Susan didn't understand, but then again Jess never told her the entire story. "Susan, I'm not talking a few thousand dollars, I'm talking close to one hundred thousand dollars."

"What?" Susan clasped her arm. "How? You've never spent money like that."

"Ned did it." The taste of defeat filled Jess and it tasted like garbage.

"You said Ned ran up some bills but I never thought it was that bad."

"It is. I won't have Hunter thinking I'm like his ex-wife, only after him for his money." Her shoulders slumped at the weight of the situation. Even if she did tell Hunter, he'd want to pay it off. There had to be another way. Before she come to the ranch she'd thought she considered every option, but now maybe it was time to explore them again.

"You're being a coward."

"Believe what you want." Jess wouldn't let Susan's opinion change her mind. She had to be strong.

A knock on Jess's front door startled her. "What is this, Grand Central Station?" She marched to her front door and threw it open.

Cal stood there, hat-in-hand and his expression grim. Her heart seized. *Hunter.*

"What's wrong, Cal?" Susan asked.

"Chris sent me. He took Hunter in to see doc and they're now on their way to the hospital."

Jess bit her lower lip until the pain registered in her brain. "I need to go to him." Oh Lord, she had to see him one last time.

"Thanks, Cal." Susan patted her shoulder. "I'll take Jess over."

"I'll send the truck to get you." Cal turned and jogged away.

"Jess?" Susan's voice was soft.

"Oh, God, Susan." Tears welled. "I forgot to ask what was wrong." The worst case scenario played out in Technicolor before her eyes.

Her friend's brow crinkled and compassion filled her blue eyes. "I'm worried too, but everything will be okay."

"Why does everyone say that? It isn't true." Her heart hurt, but she refused to let it stop her from seeing Hunter one last time.

An hour later, Jess paced in the small hospital waiting room. When she and Susan arrived, the antiseptic smell of the hospital overwhelmed Jess and she'd run back outside for some air. After some deep breaths and a self-pep talk, she found Susan waiting for her inside.

The nurse had told them the doctor was still evaluating Hunter and if they'd go into the waiting room, the doctor would update them as soon as he could. But so far, nothing. Jess glanced at the clock on the wall, then her watch. Only two minutes had passed since the last time she'd looked.

She gazed out the grimy window. Clouds had gathered in the sky, matching her gloomy mood. How much longer was it going to be? She needed to know.

"He'll be okay," Susan said for what seemed the hundredth time.

"Then why won't they tell us anything?" Jess didn't even glance at her friend.

"The doctor wants to make sure before he comes and speaks to us," Chris said, entering the room.

"What happened, Chris?" Jess asked facing him.

"Hunter started to go after you and his knee buckled."

"Just his knee?" Susan asked.

"I thought so until Doc insisted on doing a full work up."

"Did the bull catch his knee?" She fought back the tears that threatened.

"Don't think so." Chris places his hand on her shoulder. "He hit the ground pretty hard, but not on his knee."

"Then why couldn't he walk? Why did he ride that darn bull?"

"Bull riding is a part of him. If you can't accept it, then it's better you leave," Chris said.

"Chris!" Susan turned to him. "I can't believe you said that."

"He's right." Her voice was steady and calm. "He's not saying anything I'm not thinking."

"Jess, Hunter loves you. I know he does." Susan stomped over to her.

"It doesn't matter." It wouldn't last, not when she couldn't deal with her fear.

"But it does." Susan touched her hand. "I've never seen Hunter so happy as he's been with you."

"He's not happy now. He's hurt. And me, with my fears and burden? I'll only hurt him worse. Hell, he'd probably even give up his dreams for me. I won't do that to him." Jess moved away from her friend as pain crawled through her veins.

"Does Hunter know you're afraid?" Chris asked.

"No."

Before Chris could say another word the doctor walked into the room. Chris turned to him. "Doc, how's Hunter?"

"He'll be fine. X-rays were clean. He pulled a muscle and has a couple of bruised ribs. No concussion, so that's a plus. I think the shock of pain caused him to lose consciousness for a couple of seconds, but he's come to, and is going to be fine."

Jess sank onto the plastic chair. Hunter was all right. Tears of relief slipped down her face. "When can we see him?"

"You must be Jess." The doctor walked over to her. "He's been asking for you. I'll take you to him."

Jess took a deep breath and stood.

"Give him a chance." Susan gave her a hug before Jess followed the doctor down a long hallway. She heard Hunter before she stepped into the doorway.

"I can button my own shirt," he grumbled as he pushed the nurse's hands away.

Jess stared at Hunter, taking in every nuance of expression on his face. The way his eyes narrowed against the pain, the worry lines on his forehead, and the way his chin jutted up.

Relief at seeing him up and complaining made her knees weak. She almost threw herself into his arms to beg him never to climb on another bull, but she didn't. No, she wouldn't do that to him. As soon he was healed, she'd leave the Double K and him.

"Jess." His brown eyes softened when he saw her, and he held his hand out to her. The nurse left the room.

"Hey there, cowboy." She took his hand and brought it to her face loving the texture of his skin against hers.

"I'm okay, sweetheart."

"I know. The doctor told me, pulled muscles and a couple of bruised ribs." Seeing him so determined to dress himself pushed most of her fears away for the moment.

"But you're still scared." He cupped her cheek.

"Yes." She wouldn't lie.

"It was a freak accident. Normally when I ride, nothing happens."

"An accident that could have cost you your life." She didn't want to talk about his fall, to dwell on what had almost happened.

He entwined his fingers with hers and squeezed. Determination was etched into his features. "I take every precaution when I ride. Accidents happen, and sometimes someone is badly injured or killed." He shook his head when she opened her mouth. "I could be killed or hurt by driving my truck, or crossing the street, or fixing a fence on the ranch. I can't promise you another accident won't happen, no one can."

"I know." Tears filled her eyes.

"I do promise not to take risky chances." Their gazes met. " I love you, Jess."

"Oh, Hunter." The tears spilled over as she bowed her head. He loved her. Elation filled her and then depression. His declaration of love would make leaving him so much harder, but she had to do it. For him. For her. She couldn't just leave him, not right now, not while he was hurt. She could afford a few more weeks before she had to leave.

"I didn't tell you to make you cry." The pad of his thumb wiped away her tears.

"I'm crying because I'm happy." Okay, so that time she lied. She couldn't tell him the real reason for the tears, not when he was hurt.

****

Two weeks later, Hunter woke to darkness. He reached for Jess only to find empty space. He sat up frowning. Since his accident Jess hadn't been the same. She was more closed off than he'd ever seen her.

Gone was the easygoing woman he knew and loved. In her place was a stoic, uptight woman. The one who pushed him away and put up emotional walls. This was what she'd been like when they first met. He'd been patient with her, but tonight they would talk and get to the bottom of what bothered her.

He climbed out of bed and sauntered across the room to look out the window. Yep, there was Jess, standing outside in the moonlight. He slipped out the French doors, up behind her, and snagged her around the waist.

"What's wrong?"

"I didn't mean to wake you." While she didn't move out of his embrace, he could feel the mental walls between them in her stiff stance.

"You didn't." Why was she keeping him at an emotional distance? He glanced up at the star filled sky. Stress and fear was eating her from the inside out. She might think she was hiding it, but he was aware of it.

"Come back to bed," he whispered turning her in his arms. It was then he saw the sheen of tears in her eyes. His heart pounded.

"I can't sleep."

"So we don't sleep." When she didn't even smile, he figured he had to try to get at what was eating her. "Will you tell me what's bothering you?"

Her slender shoulders lifted in a careless shrug. "Old fears. Old memories."

"About?" He gathered her close, willing her to accept his strength as her own.

She stayed silent.

Hunter took her face between his hands, staring at her beautiful features. Her skin was cool to his touch. "You can talk to me. Nothing you say will change the way I feel about you. I love you. I want to be with you. I need to be with you. Don't shut me out."

A shudder shook her frame, and she lowered her eyes. Dang it, she wasn't going to answer him.

"It's..." She wrinkled her nose. "This isn't easy for me to talk about."

"We've got all night." He swept her into his arms and strode over to one of the chaise lounges by the pool. He sat, cradling her in his lap. Gathering her close, her forehead rested against his shoulder and she sighed.

"You remember when I told you my dad died when I was eighteen?" The words came out softly.

"Yes."

"My dad was a rodeo cowboy."

His arms tightened around her. Well, that explained a lot.

"When I was little I loved seeing the cows, goats, sheep and horses. I was fascinated by the cowboys, they were so big, tall, and friendly."

"So you liked us country boys even then." No wonder she fit in on the ranch so well.

"Yes." She turned her head so her cheek laid against his shoulder and snuggled closer to him. "As I grew up I noticed more and more the danger of the circuit, but Dad loved it so. He was so excited that day." Her breath brushed his skin. "I was leaving for college in a few weeks. Dad was so proud, he waved at me from the chute before he climbed on the back of a bull."

Hunter swore silently. Oh Lord, he could see where this was going.

"We all cheered until Dad was bucked off the bull." Her voice cracked.

"I'm sorry, sweetheart." No wonder she'd panicked when he rode. If only he'd known, he could have prepared her.

"He was trampled by the bull before the clowns could get to him." Her tears burned his skin and her body trembled in his embrace.

"You don't have to say anymore." He couldn't stand her pain. It wasn't fair she had to witness her father's passing.

"No, I have to finish." She sniffled. "I was hysterical. Nothing anyone could say or do would calm me down. It wasn't until later I realized my mother was as bad off as I was." She took a shuddering breath. "She tried to be brave for me and my brother, but I saw her pain. I buried my pain and took charge. Dad was gone and there was nothing I could do to bring him back. Mom and my brother needed me and I wasn't going to let them down."

Hunter rubbed her back, giving her as much comfort as he could. He didn't know what to say.

"It wasn't until two weeks later we learned Dad hadn't saved any money." Her sad laugh tugged at his heart. "He'd been winning all year, but he spent the money as soon as it came in. We were broke."

This time he swore out loud. He'd met plenty of rodeo cowboys who did the same thing, but they were single. All the married guys were very careful to send money home.

Jess shivered. "Let it all out, sweetheart." He held her tight.

"Ben, my brother, was only sixteen. Mom was a wreck and I was due at college."

"What did you do?"

"One of our neighbors kept tabs on Mom and Ben after I left. I took a part-time job while in college and sent every bit of money I could home. Ben took a job as well, even though I didn't want him to."

"And your mom?"

"She lasted a month after Ben's high school graduation before the grief finally became too much for her. At least, that's how I see it. She took off, leaving us alone."

"Oh, baby." He held her close as she sobbed. If only he'd known all this before he'd gotten on that bull. He still would have ridden, but he wouldn't have had her there watching.

"I'm sorry," she said several minutes later, raising her head to gaze up at him.

"Why are you apologizing?" He dried her cheeks with his fingers. Her eyes might be red and swollen, but she was still the most beautiful woman in the world to him.

"Because I can't watch you ride."

"You don't have to." He placed his forehead against hers. He wouldn't force her to watch him ride, not knowing her story. It was probably better this way, otherwise his mind would be on her rather than his ride and not concentrating on the bull could get one injured, or killed.

"It's a part of you." Sadness tinged her voice.

"Yes, but so are you. I don't want you to watch me ride if it's going to cause you anxiety."

"Thank you." She snuggled against him.

The quiet contentment in her voice dispelled the last of his doubts, at least for now. They could work out any problems as a team.

"Ready to go back to bed?" he whispered, his lips caressing her ear.

"Not yet." Jess sat up, straddling his hips. "The night sky is beautiful." She tilted her head back, but not before he caught a glimpse of sadness.

"No more than the woman in my arms." He ran his palms over her flat stomach to her breasts trying to erase the sorrow he'd seen in her eyes.

"Are you flirting with me, cowboy?"

The lightness of her tone let him know he managed to distract her. "More than flirting, city girl." His fingers caressed her nipples until they hardened.

"So I feel." She wiggled against his erection.

"Keep that up and we'll never make it to bed."

"Who says we have to." Sliding her hands down her body, she curled her fingers into the hem of her night gown, then pulled it up and off.

His erection went from hard to raging. She wiggled down his body, her fingers finding the elastic of his shorts. She peeled them down, releasing his sex. Sliding down his body, she pushed the fabric off his feet.

"You still have yours." Desire flared in his veins. He'd never get enough of this woman.

"Not for long." She wiggled and within seconds her panties were off and joined his on the concrete. Then she crawled up his body.

Their lips met in a dizzying kiss as the night air caressed his skin. This woman could make him lose control.

She broke the kiss and grinned at him. "I want you." Her fingers encircled his shaft.

"Ride me," he whispered. His palms framed her hips as she aligned herself, then sank down. They both moaned.

"So hard." She breathed against his skin

"So wet."

"Only for you." Their lips met as she rose.

Keeping his hands on her hips, he helped her ride him until she cried out her satisfaction into the night air. Only then did Hunter take his.

"I'm so glad you came into my life," he whispered when she collapsed against him.

CHAPTER ELEVEN

Jess yawned as she gathered up the folders she need to re-file.

"Did we have a late night last night?" Susan teased.

Heat flared in her face. After she and Hunter had made love by the pool, he'd carried her to bed and loved her again. Jess was building up memories because she needed to leave soon. She'd started to pack a few thing, but her heart was a little harder to close up and seal shut.

"You don't have to answer." Susan smiled. "That's what happens when you're in love."

Oh, yeah, she was in love with Hunter all right, but she couldn't let him know it. If he knew, he would make it impossible for her to leave. It was going to be difficult enough to give up her rough, sexy cowboy.

But for his sake she had to leave. Her trial period ended tomorrow. The bonus money would sustain her and her creditors until she found another job.

"I'm glad you decided to stay. Have you told Hunter about your finances?"

"I can't."

"Why not?"

"It's my problem." Jess paced around her office. "He'd only think I'm like Shana and after his money." Not that she hadn't thought about talking to Hunter about her situations, but each time she attempted to bring up the subject, shame held her back. Shame and fear of seeing his love disintegrate before her eyes. "I don't want him to think I'm just another woman after his bank balance. It's better this way." Also, she couldn't watch him ride bulls. And sitting at home while he rode would be even worse. She didn't want to lose the love of her life to a rodeo bull.

"What drivel. I know my brother, Jess. You and Shana, and other women who wanted his money, are worlds apart."

Jess laughed. "What about the deal I struck?"

"Deal?"

"Remember the bonus money for this job."

"Oh, that." Susan waved her hand. "That's part of the job, it has nothing to do with anything else."

"Will Hunter see it that way?" Doubt gnawed at her stomach. Was she any better than his ex-wife for striking such a one-sided deal? Yes, this was money she'd earned, but would that be enough to convince Hunter?

"He wouldn't have made the bet with you if he didn't consider it part of the job. You've earned the bonus money. You've done a terrific job."

Jess appreciated Susan's words but wished she shared Susan's confidence about how Hunter considered the deal. "Susan, you've kept my secret this long, please keep it a little longer. The less Hunter knows the better." Hunter had his own dreams to follow, and she wouldn't stand in his way.

"I don't like it. Hunter loves you."

"I don't want his love to change to hate." Jess

sighed as her shoulders slumped.

"Hunter could never hate you."

"Yes, he could. I barely like myself at times."

"What Ned did to you wasn't your fault, Jess." Susan placed a hand on her shoulder.

"I was stupid enough to believe his lies. There is no one else to blame."

"You're going to break my brother's heart."

Her breath caught in her throat. The last thing she wanted to do was hurt Hunter, but leaving was the only way to contain and minimize the damage she caused. If Hunter found out she planned to go, he'd do everything he could to prevent it. Including giving up his dream. She wouldn't let him do that, not even for her.

"It will break his heart more to give up his dreams." Jess glanced at her friend. "Chris told me Hunter has a very good chance of winning the title this year."

"Yes."

"In order to do that, he'll have to go back on the circuit for at least two months." Fear almost choked her. "I can't let him give up his chance due to my fear. He deserves to have his title and I won't have him worrying about me and my issues."

"You're underestimating my brother and the love he has for you."

"I'm doing this because I love him." Jess fought back the tears. There would be plenty of time for crying later.

"Jess," Susan started, reaching for her.

"No." Jess put her hand up in the stop position. "I

don't want to discuss this anymore."

"Stubborn," Susan muttered as she stomped out of the office. Jess sank onto the chair and covered her face. She could do this, because she had no other choice.

****

The next day, Hunter walked into the office via the back door. He couldn't wait to corner Jess for a kiss. Maybe he could convince her into canceling the meeting with the Breeding Association to go riding with him.

He'd pack a picnic lunch; take her out by the lake. After they ate, he'd go down on one knee and ask her to marry him. He patted the ring box in his pocket. He wanted his ring on her finger before he went back out on the circuit and won his title.

Striding into her small office, he stopped in disappointment. She wasn't there. Probably went to get a cup of coffee. He'd kept her up most of last night. He couldn't get enough of her.

Her trial period as office manager ended today and of course she had the job. She was a whiz at running the office and keeping everyone in line. He sauntered over to her desk and sat. While he was here he might as well print out the records he'd need for this afternoon's meeting, just in case.

He glanced at the file open on Jess's computer. Yep, she was good. The Breeders Association shouldn't have an issue with the new breeding program he wanted to try. Jess had worked out all the pros and cons of it. He leaned back in her chair while he waited for the file to print.

After he won his bull riding title, he'd settle down on the ranch with Jess. They'd have some kids and watch the ranch and his breeding program grow. The print icon flashed off and he closed the file.

Another file on the screen, one he hadn't seen before. This was financial data, and rarely did Jess pull up the finances on the ranch. She'd told him that she'd prefer if he or Chris did that.

His gut tightened as his gaze ran down the columns of numbers. When he reached the bottom he scrolled back up and scanned the file again. Credit cards maxed to the limit, several bank loans, student loans. The total was astronomical.

What had she done with all that money? Yes, school was expensive, but she'd told him she had grants that paid off most of her college and part of her brother's, so who's debt was this? What did she need so much money for?

Gambling? Drugs? He'd seen no evidence of either in her time here. His hand shook as he pulled it through his hair. What was Jess hiding?

Was she more like Shana than he knew? No. He shook his head. Jess never asked him about money or how much the ranch made. But all the records were there for her to see. And there was the case of the bonus.

Had he been a fool all this time? He shook his head. There had to be a reasonable explanation for this. If there was, why hadn't she come to him? Especially since she'd told him about her father spending all their money.

Did she fear he wouldn't understand? Then he

remembered a couple of the phone calls he'd overheard. She kept telling him it was personal and her problem. Well, she was about to learn her problems were also his. He could pay off her debts.

And there lay the problem. Jess hadn't asked him. She was too stubborn for her own good. Too proud. He'd sit her down tonight and have it out with her. He decided to scroll through her spreadsheet so he'd have the whole picture.

His fingers froze on the mouse when he saw the next page. These account numbers and amounts he was familiar with. They were his and the ranches.

"Son of a...." He pushed back from the desk. Jess was playing him for the fool, only interested in his money. Anger surged in his veins. Well, she wasn't going to get away with it.

He erased his and the ranch's information, save the sheet and closed it. He was a fool. He'd trusted her. Made himself vulnerable and this was her way of paying him back. Thank goodness he'd found this out now rather than after he asked her to marry him.

"Hunter, the Breeding Association group is here," Susan said. He glanced up to see his sister in the doorway. "Are you okay?"

"No." He stood fighting to control his anger. "Where is Jess?"

"In the conference room making sure everything is set up." Susan tilted her head and studied her brother. "What's wrong?"

"Did you know that Jess was in debt up to hear eardrums?"

His sister's cheeks turned pink.

"Oh, thank goodness she finally told you. I hated not telling you."

"She didn't tell me." He clenched his teeth.

"Crap. How did you find out?"

"Doesn't matter. Why didn't you tell me? I'm your brother, for God's sake." Looks like Jess had played him for a fool using his sister as a shield.

"It wasn't my secret to tell."

"I'm your brother." He managed to bit back his words about her loyalty to family.

His baby sister's eyes grew wide. "Yes. I was giving Jess time to figure out how to handle the problem and how to tell you."

He stood. "She handled it all right." By playing him. Why hadn't he'd seen through her sooner? Her hot and cold moods. After Shana, why hadn't he recognize it?

"Hunter." Susan touched his arm.

"Hey, you two. Everyone is ready," Chris called down the hallway.

"We're coming," Susan yelled, then she looked back at him.

"Let it go, Susan." He pushed by her and marched to the conference room. "Good afternoon," he said, nodding to everyone with a smile, until he got to Jess. His smile faded and his fingers curled into his palms. Meeting first, then he'd deal with her.

The Breeding Association meeting finished up and everyone was happy, except him. He'd told her to meet him in his office in ten minutes and here she was.

"You wanted to see me," Jess said standing in the

doorway of his office.

"Come in and sit down." He studied her. There was puzzlement on her face.

"Is there something wrong?" She lowered her willowy form onto the chair, folding her hands in her lap.

Her fragility yanked at his gut. It was all an act. "Yes, you could say that." His fingers tapped against the wood grain of his desktop.

"And?" A frown marred her forehead.

Her confusion threw him. Maybe Susan was right and Jess wanted to tell him. But why hadn't she? She'd had plenty of time. No. He hardened his heart. She was only after his money, like all the other women he'd been with.

"I think this says it all." He picked up the check from his desk and dangled it in front of her.

Her hand shook as she took it. She read the check and the color drained from of her face. "What is the meaning of this?"

"It's a check." He stared at her.

"I know what it is." She shook her head. "Why are you giving it to me?"

Hunter forced down his compassion and stood. "It's the bonus you were promised at the beginning of the job. Now that your trial has passed you can leave."

"Excuse me?" Jess couldn't comprehend what Hunter was saying.

"I don't need your services anymore." He strode around the desk. "In or out of bed."

She recoiled in shock. Did he just imply... Jess glanced up at his face. His chocolate eyes were cold and his jaw clenched. "What the hell is wrong with you?"

"Never leave anything lying around you don't want others to see." He reached behind him, picked up a piece of paper and thrust it into her hand.

Jess stared at the paper in her hand. What the heck? How did he get this? She kept all her personal files password encoded to be safe. "This." The paper crinkled in her fist. "Is none of your business."

"You lied to me." He gripped her by shoulders. "Did you think if we slept together I'd pay off those bills for you?"

The paper dropped from her hand before she pulled out of his hold and stepped back...the crack of her hand against his cheek was loud in the silence.

"How dare you." Her voice shook, along with her body. Her shoulders slumped and her worst fear had just come true. But she was a fighter. She'd hoped he'd give her the benefit of the doubt, but no one ever had so why should she think he could be any different.

"I dare because it's true." He rubbed his cheek, scowling.

"I would never use sex to gain money."

"So, did I screw up your plan by taking you to my bed? Were you just planning on stringing me along until I married you? Then you could take half my assets in the divorce?" He stepped back. "Sorry, city girl, but you wouldn't get crap."

"I'd never marry a cowboy." The words were out of her mouth before she could stop them.

Hunter stiffened as the coldness in his eyes spread over him.

"You have until tomorrow morning to get off my ranch." He marched out of the room.

Jess was frozen in place. She opened her mouth to call him back, then shut it. He wasn't going to listen to her, no matter what she said. He believed she was just like his ex. She reached down and picked the paper off the floor, before smoothing it out.

Hell. She must have left her spreadsheet up on the computer, because not only was her information there but the ranch financials. She'd been using them as a template. Was this what he'd seen? She started to go after him but stopped at his office door. Hunter wasn't going to listen to her. Now she had to pick up the shattered pieces of her life once again.

Squaring her shoulders, strode out of Hunter's office and back to her cottage. Well, not hers anymore. She surveyed the space that had been her home. Despair settled over her. She had a lot of packing to do.

An hour later, Susan arrived. "So you're just going to leave?" Susan snapped her finger at Jess.

"Hunter wants me gone." Thank goodness she'd kept the boxes from when she moved in three months ago. Was that all it was? So much in her life had changed in a short period of time. And yet she was right back where she started. Worse now, because she'd lost the love of her life.

"And you're just giving up?"

Jess finished taping the box shut, straightened and stared at her friend. "He believes I'm just like his ex. After his money."

"Did you explain to him about Ned?"

"What difference would it make?" She turned away from Susan's searching gaze. Tears clogged her throat as she stared at the white wall still bearing the small holes from her art work.

The irony of it all was that the fear she'd felt about keeping her job and avoiding the bulls was nothing compared to the loss and grief swamping her now. She thought she'd hit every low know to woman-kind, but no, she was now sitting on her butt at the rock bottom.

Stop feeling sorry for yourself.

"Darn stubborn man." Susan touched her arm. "You can stay with me."

Jess shook her head, fighting against the sympathy her friend offered because it led straight to self-pitting tears. Ridiculous. She'd seen her father killed by a bull. She'd been hit with more bills that she'd ever imagined. So she'd been through much worse thing than having her heart torn out. Why did this feel so much worse?

Her stomach churned with fear, dread and more. With eyes stinging from holding back tears, Jess faced her friend. "Hunter needs you. If you side with me, he'll feel more betrayed than he already does."

"I should go knock some sense into my brother."

Jess managed a laugh. Her self-control made her proud. She patted Susan's hand. "Don't. That won't help me and would only hurt your relationship with him."

"All right, for the moment." Susan picked up a box. "I don't like it, but I'll help you pack. Otherwise you'll be up all night."

"Thanks." Not that she planned on sleeping tonight.

The next morning, Jess stifled a yawn as she waited for the movers to arrive. Thank goodness they weren't busy. All night, she'd tossed and turned over what had happened between her and Hunter. Would Hunter feel different if she told him about Ned's actions? She didn't know. She didn't want Hunter to feel obligated to help her out. Which was why she crept into the office early this morning and put the check on his desk.

Yes, she'd earned it for the job she did at the office, but her pride refused to take it. Not when he believed what he did.

A pounding on the door brought her out of her musings. The moving guys were here. Good. It was time to leave. She pulled the door open.

A six-foot tower of muscle and steaming anger greeted her. "Haven't you done enough without involving my sister?" Hunter demanded, reminding her of a raging bull.

His lips pressed together, his hat pulled down practically covering his eyes, and the lines of tiredness on his face. Why did she have to fall in love with this cowboy? Her heart broke into more pieces.

"I have no idea of what you're talking about." She sighed.

"Really? Susan marched over to my place after helping you pack last night." He hit the door frame. "She could have been a damn lawyer."

Jess just stared at Hunter. "Fine, you want to believe I sent Susan over to you, then believe it. Are you happy now?" She rubbed her temples. "I'm sorry I disrupted your life. I never meant to hurt you."

"Why don't I believe that?" The coldness in his voice caused ice to form in her veins. She'd had enough.

"I'm not asking for your forgiveness, so let's just drop the subject." The rumble of a truck had her mentally saying a prayer of thanks. "Movers are here. I'll be out of your way soon."

"I knew you couldn't leave it alone, Hunter," Susan said, marching up the walkway.

Jess rolled her eyes. She really didn't need this right now. "Susan..."

"Jess is the best thing that's ever happened to you and this ranch. Can't you see she's nothing like Shana?" Susan ranted.

"This is between Jess and I. Stop butting in," Hunter calmly said to his sister.

"Men." Susan threw her hands into the air.

Hunter shook his head and strode away.

"If you'd open your eyes, you'd see a good woman standing in front of you!" Susan yelled at his retreating figure.

Jess stood frozen, praying for the strength to get through the day. The movers pulled up and she pasted on a smile on her face. Now she'd get on with her life such as it was. Alone.

CHAPTER TWELVE

Jess shut her Oklahoma apartment door, kicked off her shoes, and sorted through her mail. Bills, bills and more bills. They followed her everywhere. But the Rodeo News magazine caught her eye. Dropping everything else onto the table, she took the magazine over to the sofa and sank down into the cushions. Two months since she left Hunter and there wasn't a minute she didn't missed him.

She grabbed the TV remote and turned on the sports channel. She flipped through the magazine. No pictures. Tossing it aside, she glanced at the TV. Who knew she'd be reduced to this. Pathetic. And she really didn't have time to sit here and feel sorry for herself. Maggie, her boss and newfound friend, would arrive any minute so she better get a move on.

Her gaze strayed to the TV. Lord, she was weak, but she just wanted a morsel of news to reassure herself Hunter was okay.

The announcer said they'd have rodeo highlights after the commercial, so Jess sat waiting. The commercial faded and Hunter's picture came up. Jess moved closer to the screen. Her fingers tracing the wrinkles on his forehead, before the picture disappeared.

"Hunter Knight has won another first place finish."

Her breath caught in her throat. She was so proud of him. "After a nasty fall earlier this year—"

She tried to concentrate on the announcer's words.

"—some wondered if he'd return. Well, Knight is back with a vengeance. His determination is phenomenal. We'll be keeping an eye on this bull rider. And now on to football."

Jess rose to her feet and was surprised when a tear hit her hand. She was crying. She brushed the tears away, but more arrived. Oh, Lord, just seeing him on the TV screen made her one hot mess.

The door-bell pealed and she jumped a mile. Grabbing several tissues, she tried to mop her face before she opened the door.

"Honey, what happened?" Alarm filled Maggie's eyes beneath the mop of curly dark hair.

Jess tried to smile. "It's fine. Sad commercial." Maggie was a godsend. Jess had answered an ad Maggie put out for an office manager. Maggie took her under her wing when she applied for the job and they'd become friends.

"Right." Maggie held up a bag. "I hope you like Chinese." Maggie set down her carry-everywhere briefcase before she brushed past Jess into her small kitchen.

"I'm not very hungry." She should have guessed Maggie would bring food when she said she was coming over for some girl talk.

"If you don't eat soon, a strong gust of wind is going to blow you away."

Delicious scents of fried rice, broccoli and beef,

almond chicken and egg rolls made her stomach let out a growl. "Let's eat." Within minutes they were seated at the small kitchen table, plates piled high.

"Want to tell me about the man you're mooning over?" Maggie asked before taking a bite of her food.

"I don't know what you're talking about." The food she'd stuck in her mouth turned to dust.

"I know man trouble when I see it. Would it have anything to do with Ned Miles?"

"What? How did you hear that name?" The fork in her hand began to shake, then her body. She hadn't told Maggie anything about why she was in Oklahoma. Shame, stupidity, and gullibility were not good qualities for an office manager. *Back up. That woman was gone, remember.*

"Oh honey, what kind of trouble are you in?"

"What do you mean?" Jess lowered her gaze from the concern in Maggie's eyes.

"I received an interesting phone call right before I left the office today."

Oh, God, someone had tracked her down again. "Are you going to fire me?" Fear trickled up her spine. She was finally making progress. Was it all going to hell in a hand basket?

"I'm your friend as well as your employer. I can help you, but you have to reach out. What is going on?"

Jess let out a breath. What did she have to lose? She already lost Hunter, the love of her life. What's with losing a little dignity too? "It's complicated."

"Tell me." Maggie covered Jess's hand with hers. "I'm a lawyer, remember."

"Yes." Jess stood and began pacing. "But this isn't your problem."

"No, but it's obviously causing you a lot of turmoil. I can only help you if you tell me what's going on."

Tears filled her eyes again. The concern in Maggie's voice was her undoing. Jess had shouldered this burden for too long and it was easier to hold it together when she was alone.

After shedding a few tears, Jess poured her heart out to Maggie. She held nothing back, telling her about Ned, the debt, leaving LA, about the Double K and about Hunter.

"You've really had a bad time of it." Maggie stood, grabbed her briefcase and pulled out a legal pad. "Way to bad a time. Now let's fix it."

"How?" She took a sip of the water Maggie had thrust into her hand. The cool liquid washing away the dryness in her throat.

"First, we prove those charges weren't made by you and then we go after that forgery of your name on loan papers." Maggie wrote something down on the paper in front of her. "The man committed fraud and he's going to pay for it."

"I can't prove any of it."

"But I can. Welcome to my world. Did you never think about seeing a lawyer?"

Jess shook her head. "I figured it was just my word against his. Not to mention I didn't have the money to spare to hire a lawyer."

"I'm so glad you told me all this." Maggie patted the back of her hand. "The bank will have to produce the loan paperwork with signatures. I can use a handwriting expert to prove it's not your signature. Then there's all the charges he's done since you left Los Angeles."

"What about the debt collectors who say I have no choice but to pay the money?" Did she dare hope there was a way out of this mess?

"Those vultures. They say that all the time. They'll say anything to get their money."

Fresh tears threatened. "I was really stupid about all this."

"Not stupid. Uninformed and caught up in a situation you didn't make. Even in this day and age a lot of people don't understand their rights. But lucky for you, you have me."

"Do you really think you can beat this?" Hope flickered in her belly. If she could get the creditors off her back, get this mess cleaned up, maybe, finally, she'd be able to breathe. To smile again. Then she remembered the anger in Hunter's face, in his voice. Maybe she could see him and show him she was free of debt, that she wasn't like his ex just after his money.

"Yes. Now start giving me details of everything."

****

Hunter ran a hand through his hair. This new office manager was not working out like he'd hoped. The man was slower than a snail, constantly asked questions, and supposedly was an experienced ranch hand. Hunter had his doubts. If he wasn't on the phone straightening out some mess the guy caused, then he was in his office or on the phone with Chris or

Susan.

When Jess was here everything had run smoothly and he'd never had to worry. She never missed a thing, even when he'd forgotten a bill or shipment. She was always there with a reminder.

He glanced up at the canvas on his wall. When he hired the new office manager he'd gone over to the cottage. He'd found the canvas propped up against the wall with his name on it. His heart jumped a beat when he picked it up and looked at it.

Jess had painted him riding Thunder. He didn't know when or how she'd captured then together, but it was the perfect vision of man and horse. The painting showed a labor of love and hard work. He'd accused Jess of being a party girl, but it wasn't true. Oh, she had a wild side to her, but she was a woman of deep passion and commitment. And the painting showed how much she understood the spirit of ranching, and his spirit.

He swung his office chair around and faced his computer. There had to be an explanation for her debt and why she'd been looking at the ranch's financials? Now that his anger had faded, he began to look at things logically. She hadn't even defended herself when he accused her. She'd fought with him to get the job, bargaining with him, yet she'd left her bonus check on his desk. Things were not adding up.

Fear gnawed at him, driving him to look for answers. What if he was wrong? His fingers clicked on the mouse, bringing up the files and began to compare them. Within seconds he saw his answer. He'd reacted out of character because he was afraid,

Jess had wormed her way into his heart.

"Susan!"

"You bellowed, my bull-headed brother?" Susan said as she sashayed into his office a minute later.

"How did Jess get into debt?"

"You have all the answers, remember?" She crossed her arms over her chest and stared at him.

His sister was right to be mad at him, hell he was mad at himself. "Have you heard from Jess?"

"I wouldn't tell you if I had."

"Don't blame you one bit, but I was wrong."

"It's about darn time you admitted it." Susan sank down onto the chair in front of his desk. "What changed your mind?"

"Several things. She didn't even argue with me when I accused her of being a gold-digger. Then she left her bonus check. Thing weren't adding up."

"So what makes you think I know anything?"

"Well, you ripped me a new one after Jess left, let alone you being barely able to tolerate my presence. And you are her best friend."

"Jess was a pawn in Ned's life." Susan leaned forward. "You hurt her, Hunter, even more so than that scum Ned. She loved you."

"I never meant to hurt her." Yet, he had. He'd hurt her in more ways than one because he hadn't been able to let go of that city-girl chip on his shoulder. He knew that now. Hunter needed to find Jess. He would eat crow to make it up to her, because he'd been wrong. And he missed her. He loved her. "Help me Susan, I need her. I love her."

"You need to tell Jess you love her."

"I will, just help me find her."

"I'll do my best, but first, here's the lowdown on her debts."

As Hunter listened to his sister, his blood boiled. How dare this Ned take advantage of Jess's good nature. And why hadn't Jess come to him, or at least to Susan? It angered him that she hadn't, but then again, he could understand pride and shame.

When his sister was done, he said, "How do I find her?"

****

A month later, Jess took a deep breath and let it out. She was free. It was over. "I can't believe it," she whispered to Maggie.

"Believe." Maggie squeezed her hand.

Ned had been caught red-handed in his forgeries and when Maggie asked the judge for a summary judgment, it was granted. Even though California was a community property State, Jess had never married Ned. And she'd already paid more than her fair share of the debts. Ned was in jail in California and Jess had her life back.

It would take time before her credit report was cleaned up, but at least she wouldn't have creditors calling her all the time.

"Let's go celebrate," Maggie said as they walked out of the courthouse.

"Not tonight." Jess's nerves had been stretched to the limit. She wanted to go home and collapse. "I'm exhausted."

"All right, but next week we celebrate. I'll see you Monday morning." Maggie strode away.

Jess turned and took her time walking home, only about a mile away. She needed some time alone, time to sort out what she was going to do next. Once inside her apartment, she pulled out the letter Maggie had given her earlier.

A smile crept over her face. She didn't know how Susan had done it, but she'd managed to track Jess down. Well, as much as she could. The letter had gone to Maggie. This was the third letter in the last two weeks. Time to call her friend and tell her everything was okay.

She poured herself a cup of tea, then sat down on the sofa and picked up the phone. It was Friday and Hunter would be on his way to the next rodeo. She dialed.

"Double K," said a male voice.

The words died in her throat. Hunter's voice. Her heart pounded. Goosebumps crawled up her arms. It was almost as if they were in the same room together.

"Hello? Is anyone there?"

Her mouth opened, but nothing came out. Why did he have to answer the phone? Where was Susan? Dang it, she should have called Susan at her house and not at the office.

"Jess?"

Had she made a noise? Her hand trembled. She wanted to answer him, but she couldn't. Fear filled her.

"Wrong number," the words came out in a whisper.

"Oh God, Jess. Don't hang up. Talk to—"

His words cut off as she hung the receiver up.

Cold shivers racked her body and she wrapped her arms around her stomach. Why did it hurt so much to hear his voice after all this time? *Because I still love him.*

The anger which had sustained her all this time was absent. Her money issues were gone now. Maybe it was time to stop running. Because that's what she'd done. She'd run from Hunter instead of confronting him and explaining. She ran because she was ashamed and prideful. She'd planned on talking to him once her debts were cleared up, so why was she so reluctant?

Time to pull up her big girl panties and go after her man. She looked at the calendar. Thanksgiving was in a week and then December. December. Jess rubbed her forehead. Could she do this? She didn't have a lot of time, but she'd make it work. Bouncing to her feet, she ran to her computer and began her search.

****

Jess walked around the rodeo grounds with a smile. She'd forgotten about the vendors. So many of them, selling toys for the kids, big and little, hats, chaps, fencing vendors, you name it. If it had to do with ranching or rodeo they were here.

The National Finals Rodeo in Las Vegas. A cowboy's dream. Memories of being with her family, walking around the grounds before her dad would ride, filled her mind. It had been a happy time.

She wandered up to the medical booth and was looking over a brochure when a voice said, "Jess?"

Her head jerked up to see her baby brother. "Ben." She launched herself into his arms. While they'd talked, they hadn't seen each other in almost a year.

"What are you doing here?" he asked after hugging her.

"I could ask you the same thing." She took in his bronze skin and tone body.

"Remember I told you about the EMT gig?"

"Yes." She tilted her head as she stared at him. He had made the most of his opportunities and was all grown up. Pride swelled within her.

He grinned, his teeth bright white against his tan skin. "Well, it's with the rodeo. I traveled around all summer, and was invited to come to the NFR."

"That's wonderful." She hugged him again. He'd put on muscle and filled out some since the last time she'd seen him.

"You're not mad?"

"No." She couldn't help but smile at Ben's relief. He was working behind the scenes, not riding bulls.

"Well, Ben, who's this lovely young thing?" another man asked walking up to them.

"Zack this is my sister, Jess. Jess, my boss, Zack."

"Hi, Zack." Jess held her hand out as her gaze took in Zack. Tall, blond hair, and that don't-mess-with-me look about him.

"Sister, huh?" He shook her hand. "Why didn't you say she was coming?"

"I didn't know." Ben grinned.

"Well, we need to go get ready, they're about to start. You have your seat, Jess?"

"Actually, I don't. There weren't any tickets left,

but I can wander the shopping area."

"Can she come in back with us?" Ben asked.

"Yeah, I've got just the place she can sit." Zach cupped her elbow and off they went.

When they announced that bull riding was the next event, Jess perched on the edge of her seat. True to his word, Zach got her into a seat right above the chutes in an area reserved for rodeo personnel.

She was still worried Hunter could get hurt, but she no longer let her fear control her. If she was going to have a life with him, she would learn to cope. In the two weeks between her victory in court and today, she'd badgered Maggie into giving her vacation time, bought a plane ticket, and arrived at the NFR. She was going to watch her man win his title and then see if he still wanted her around.

"Hunter Knight is next," said the announcer and her heart sped up. Hunter was at the chute. He talked with the other riders as he straddled the bull. "Hunter is in first place and as long as he can stay on the bull for eight seconds and score a seventy-five or better he'll win the title." Jess's gaze didn't stray from Hunter as he prepared himself. "After an injury earlier this year, Hunter came back with a vengeance in August. And tonight he drew Wicked, one of the rankest bulls out there."

A rank bull. Her heart lodged in her throat. But she had confidence in Hunter. He lowered himself, wrapped his hand in the rigging, then pulled his hat down tight. A slight nod of his head and the chute flew open.

The bull snorted and its hooves hit the metal gate.

The bull lunged into the area and began spinning.

Her fingers curled into her palms as she surged to her feet. "Come on Hunter, you can do it," she yelled.

With each jump and turn her heart flinched, but soon the buzzer went off and a roar went up from the crowd. The pickup men rode to Hunter and got him off the maniacal bull. Hunter slid to the dirt-packed ground, watching the bull while he strode to the side of the arena.

She kept her gaze on his face. The same joy she witnessed as a child on her father's face after a great ride lit his features. A weight lifted from her heart.

The bull was escorted from the arena and Jess took a breath. Then Hunter's score flashed. A ninety-four. Jess went wild with the crowd. He'd done it, not only a fantastic score, but he'd won his title. She jumped up and down, her gaze never leaving him as he walked to the gate. It was opened and then...wait, was that Ben? Her brother was talking to Hunter.

Hunter's head lifted, his gaze searching the stand and locked on her. He marched her way as her heart pounded. Should she go down and meet him? Before she could make a decision, he'd climbed the railing and was strutting down the row of seats wearing a determined look on his face.

She drank in his handsome face, his lean body, and his sexy smile. Without thinking, she held her hand out to him. Warmth enveloped her as his fingers closed over hers.

"About darn time you showed up, my Jess."

"Hi ya', cowboy."

Hunter's rich laughter filled the air as he pulled

her into his arms and his lips closed over hers. She clutched his shoulders for dear life as he took possession of her mouth. His tongue thrust between her lips, tangling with hers before retreating as he nipped at her lips.

When she could breathe again, she gazed into his chocolate eyes. "That's quite a welcome." There were hoots and hollers from the cowboys around them, but she ignored them.

"I'm sorry, Jess. I never should have doubted you." His arms tightened around her waist.

"And I should have explained, but it no longer matters. I'm here."

"You are, thank God. You did a great job hiding from me, city girl."

"You were looking for me even after everything?" She stroked his cheek. Her fingers picked up the hint of whiskers on his face, an appetizer to her hunger for every inch of him.

He stared deeply into her eyes, so close his breath tickled her lips. "Hell, yeah. I love you, Jess."

His words hit her like a freight train. He loved her. She smiled and lost herself into the depths of his eyes. "I love you too, cowboy."

His eyes lit up and then surprise flashed in them. "You watched me ride?" Amazement laced his voice.

"Yep, and a very impressive ride it was."

"Hey, Hunter," Chris yelled.

"What?"

"Time to get your winnings."

"Let's go." He clasped her hand.

"Hunter?"

"You're coming with me, I'm not going to lose you again." He tugged her down the stairs, to the gate where Chris waited.

"I can't go out there," Jess said. Her in front of the roaring crowd? Her insides quaked.

"Sure you can." Chris clasped Hunter's hand. "Go get your winnings."

"Thanks." Hunter slipped his free hand into his jeans pocket before he tightened his hold on Jess's waist and guided her out into the dirt arena.

****

His heart pounded, not only from his ride, but from finding her in the audience. Hell, who was he kidding? His heart had gone crazy the second he'd seen Jess. He hadn't been joking when he'd said he was going to find her. Susan had already sent letters, but they're hadn't been a reply, only her one hang-up call.

After today, he'd planned on going to the address Susan mailed the letters to, but Jess was here. And thanks to her brother, Ben, for pointing her out. Ben was a good man. He'd told Hunter that if he made his sister cry, he'd beat the crap out of him.

He had no intention of making her cry.

Anticipation filled the air. He shook hands with the rodeo personnel. Took his buckle and certificate. He would get the check later. The time had come to put his heart out there, the toughest ride of his life with the most important outcome.

He turned to Jess. He handed her the buckle and paper before he got down on one knee.

The stadium went silent with anticipation.

"Hunter?" Her amber eyes grew wide and voice shook.

"Jessica Sinclair," he stated in a clear loud voice. "I love you. Will you do me the honor of being my wife." With trembling fingers, he pulled the ring from his pocket. The one he'd been carrying ever since she'd left.

"Oh, my God." Her cheeks flushed, and the crowed oohed. Jess cleared her throat. "Hunter Knight, I would be honored to be your wife."

His chest swelled as he slipped the ring over her finger. The crowd's wild cheering faded as he stood and pulled her into his arms and sealed the proposal with a kiss.

He rested his forehead against hers and grinned. He had his life partner, the love of his life, the biggest trophy any man could ever want. Jess was the only one who mattered.

About the Author

Marie Tuhart lives in the beautiful Pacific Northwest with her muse, Penny, a four pound toy poodle. Marie loves to read and write, when she's not writing, she spends time with family, traveling and enjoying life.

Marie is a multi-published author with The Wild Rose Press, Trifecta Publishing and does some self-publishing. To be alerted on new releases follow Marie on Amazon or Book Bub. Also you can join Marie's newsletter where she gives her group advance information on her books, runs contests and does giveaways just for newsletter readers. Marie can also be found on Goodreads, Pinterest, Twitter, and Facebook.

More Information on Marie:

Website: www.marietuhart.com
Sign up for Marie's newsletter at:
http://eepurl.com/bmWUZH